# HELD

# HELD

## KIMBERLY A. BETTES

Case Publishing
USA

Case Publishing
Printed in the United States of America.
First edition: 2012

## -*MINUTES TO DEATH SERIES*-
The Loneliest Road
Close to Home
The Last Resort
Shock Rock
The French Quarter

## -*ANTHOLOGIES*-
Carnage: After the End Volume 1
Legends of Urban Horror: A Friend of a Friend Told Me

## -*ESSAYS*-
Everybody Wants to Write a Book

"I was just expecting a dark run-of-the-mill thriller and found a writer who can actually scare the heebie jeebies out of me."

———

"Brilliant start to finish. I can't believe this came from the mind of a woman."

———

"Texas Chainsaw meets Silence of the Lambs."

———

"Bettes grabs you by the throat on the first page and relentlessly squeezes you to the last."

———

"I thought I'd read the sickest books out there but this just crept to the top spot without warning."

———

"The most sick, twisted, and violent book I have ever read!"

# 1

Stepping out of the store, I squinted against the glare of the bright afternoon sunlight. As I walked across the parking lot, I went over the purchase in my mind, certain that the bubble gum-smacking cashier had overcharged me. I stepped into the narrow space between my smaller SUV and the behemoth SUV parked beside me and pulled the receipt out of my purse to study it. With my attention on the receipt, I was unaware of anyone else until I felt a gun poke into my ribs, the steel barrel causing me to wince instinctively.

He wrapped his left arm around me and squeezed my left shoulder tightly, his fingers digging into my flesh. With his right hand, he shoved the gun into my ribs even harder.

My breath caught in my chest, trapped by shocked lungs. Everything happened so fast. One second, everything was fine, normal. The next second, he was there, gun pressed to my side, pulling me against him tightly. I had no time to process the situation, no time to register the fact that nothing would ever be fine again.

To others, we looked like nothing more than a normal couple returning to our car after shopping in the mall. Even if someone had noticed the fear on my face, it might easily be mistaken for anger. Onlookers might assume we were a couple having an argument. No one could see the gun. My arm was bent at the elbow and had a shopping bag dangling from it, hiding the weapon well.

It didn't much matter what we looked like or what was hidden. There were only a handful of other people in the parking lot, none of which even glanced at us. How could they? We were hidden by the SUVs, sandwiched in between two of the largest vehicles on the market.

My mind, every bit as shocked as the rest of me, struggled to grasp the situation and find a way out of it. I thought of screaming. I thought of wrenching free of him, turning and running. But I also thought of my husband and my son. If I did any of those things, this man would shoot me. It would be easy to do. The gun was already buried in my ribcage, his finger undoubtedly on the trigger. If he didn't mean me harm, he wouldn't have the gun. He meant business. And if the pistol were equipped with a silencer, he could shoot me and be long gone before anyone even realized I was on the ground. Had the parking lot contained more people, screaming and running might've been an option. Surely he wouldn't shoot me with so many witnesses. But that wasn't the case here. Not today. Not on a stupid Tuesday afternoon.

Before I could hate myself for not waiting until later, when more people were at the mall, to shop for jeans that were supposed to be on sale but weren't because the pink haired bubble gum smacker rang them up wrong, he spoke.

"Open it," he commanded.

I dug through my purse, wishing I carried bear spray or Mace or hairspray or anything that would give me the second I needed to get away from him. But I didn't carry anything like that. I never thought I'd need it.

My fingers rummaged around at the bottom of my purse, feeling the half-empty pack of spearmint gum, the emergency tampon with the torn wrapper, the extra pacifier, my wallet, and finally my keys. I jerked them out of my purse, nearly dropped them on the ground, and clumsily began to unlock the door.

The closer we were to getting in the car, the harder he pushed on the gun. I was going to have one hell of a bruise. Assuming, that is, I lived long enough to get a bruise.

2

When my trembling hands finally managed to unlock the door, he tightened his grip on my shoulder even more, causing me to wince from the pain. He leaned into my ear, which would look to others as if he were whispering something to me. Had he whispered, I wouldn't have heard him over the sound of my pounding heart echoing in my ears.

"You're going to get in, slide over to the passenger seat, and nothing more. Do you understand?" He spoke evenly, though in a low tone to avoid being heard by anyone else who might be listening.

I didn't look at him. I couldn't. I just stood there, staring at the pavement in shock and very much afraid. My mind was racing, my thoughts a blur.

"If you do anything, and I mean anything other than what I've told you to do, I'll kill you. And if you manage to get away from me, I'll kill your family, and I'll take my sweet time doing it. Do you understand?"

This time, I nodded, quick to agree to anything that would keep my husband and son safe.

He kissed me on the cheek quickly, causing the knot in my stomach to roll.

"Good. Now get in."

He snatched the keys from me, and I did as I was told, though the urge to open the passenger side door and flee was overwhelming.

He got in quickly after me and started the vehicle. I made myself as small as possible and leaned against the door, watching out the window as we drove through the parking lot and away from my life, headed toward wherever it was we were going. Hopefully, someone I knew would see us and notice the look on my face. But I saw no one I knew.

I fought to keep from vomiting as I realized that no one was going to save me. No one was going to stop him from taking me.

If I'd just stayed home today like I had originally planned, this wouldn't have happened. But I hadn't. Damn me and my quest for discounted jeans.

The best thing that could happen to me now is he'd rape me and throw me out of the car somewhere. Knowing that was the best thing that could happen, I tried not to imagine the worst. But I knew. I knew from the moment I felt the barrel of his gun press against my ribs.

Even if I could somehow manage to escape him at some point, everything was going to be different. Assuming he didn't kill me first, life as I knew it was over and gone forever. If he stopped the car right now, told me he'd been joking and was sorry, then left and I never saw him again, everything would still be different. I'd never again park near large vehicles. I'd never let my guard down anywhere. I would constantly be aware of everything that was happening around me at all times. In essence, I'd drive myself mad trying to stay safe.

But I didn't have to worry about any of that because he wasn't stopping, and I was sure he wasn't joking.

In the side mirror, I watched as the parking lot slipped away behind me, taking me farther and farther from my life and from any hope I had of ever again seeing my husband and son.

As he drove through the city, twisting and turning through neighborhoods I'd never seen, he took many unnecessary turns. There were times when he turned right four times in a row, taking us all the way around a block and back to where we were. At first, I thought maybe he was lost. Then I realized that he was trying to confuse me so I didn't know where we were or where we were going. I took this as a good sign. If he planned to kill me right away, he wouldn't have bothered to confuse me.

For a while, I kept my eyes on the Gateway Arch, standing proudly above the St. Louis skyline. But after I realized what he was doing, I stopped using it to keep track of where we were and began just looking at it, wondering if I was seeing it for the last time.

Since it wasn't doing me any good to try to remember our route, and staring at the Arch was only making me sad, I decided to check out the man behind the wheel.

From the corner of my eye, I first noticed his shoes. They were dark brown, sort of a low-top boot type of shoe. His socks were beige. His pants were khaki. His shirt was a white long-sleeve button-down with the sleeves rolled up to his elbows. The top few buttons were undone, exposing a white undershirt and a few chest hairs.

I risked a glance at the driver. He was a big man. It wasn't that he was fat and it wasn't that he was all muscle. It was somewhere in the middle. I guessed him to be about 6'2", maybe 6'3", and he probably weighed 250 pounds or so. His hair was dark brown, bordering on black, with grey at the temples. He was cleanly shaven. His face bore no distinguishing features that stuck out or could be identifying.

Had he not kidnapped me, I might've thought him to be a handsome man. But here we were.

Though I thought I was being sneaky about stealing glances at him, he must've caught me. From his pocket, he pulled a pair of sunglasses and ordered me to put them on. I did as I was told. They were the sporty kind that wrapped around the eyes, keeping out the sunlight. But these were more than that. They didn't just keep out the natural light and block the UV rays of the sun. They kept out all light. I blinked, confused as to why I could no longer see anything more than a thin strip of light at the top and bottom of the glasses. Then I realized he had spray painted them black.

A new kind of fear gripped me. It was bad enough that he had kidnapped me. But now it seemed that he had planned it. No one carries around painted sunglasses for any other reason. He had come to the mall with a plan, and I had walked right into it.

As he continued to drive, I wondered if he had specifically planned to kidnap me or if I was just the woman who happened along at the wrong time for me, right time for him. I could think of no one I'd wronged, no enemies of mine or my husband's, and no one who'd wish to harm either of us. And moreover, I didn't know the man behind the wheel, though he did look vaguely familiar.

Finally, I felt the vehicle slow as he pulled into what I assumed was a driveway. A few seconds later, he stopped and put the SUV in park and turned off the engine.

I reached up to take off the sunglasses. He didn't stop me, so I removed them. Risking a quick glance of my surroundings, I saw that we were parked in a garage. His garage, no doubt.

In the side mirror, I saw that he'd left the door open so we could just pull in, but now he was going to have to get out and close it. If he had a remote control for it, he'd left it in his car, which was surely sitting in the parking lot of the mall.

He sat behind the wheel for a few seconds, glancing in the rearview mirrors before turning to me.

"I'm going to get out and close the door. You are to sit here and do nothing. Don't move one muscle. If you do, I'll kill you. You got that?"

I nodded.

He got out quickly, and I watched in the mirror as he shut and locked the garage door. He then hurried to my side of the SUV and opened the door.

Reaching in and grabbing my right arm with his left hand, he said, "Let's go."

I thought of refusing. If I could overpower him now, I could get out of the garage and run. But he put his right hand on the gun in the waistband of his khakis, and all thoughts of fleeing left me. I got out of the car.

Stupidly, I realized that I still had the bag from the mall hanging from my wrist. My purse was still slung over my shoulder and was clamped between my arm and my side. If only there was a way to turn those jeans into a weapon. Perhaps I could smother him with them. Or strangle him. Those were the only ways I could think of, and I knew that both would be impossible. He was bigger than me. And he had a gun.

He continued to hold my arm as he closed the car door and pulled me along behind him, walking quickly enough to cause me to jog.

We went through the door that led from the garage to the small laundry room. I saw no dirty laundry. No clean laundry. No laundry of any kind. There were lots of various cleaning products on the shelf above the washing machine and dryer, all sitting neatly, labels facing forward.

Through the laundry room, we went into the kitchen. I saw no dirty dishes. No clean dishes. No dishes of any kind. They were surely all put away, everything in its place. I saw no food. No trash. No food crumbs. No spills. No dust. No cobwebs. Nothing. There weren't even any visible grease spots on the stove. It was immaculate.

In the kitchen, he stopped suddenly and turned to me. I didn't see that he was stopping in time, and when he spun around, I bumped into him.

He stared at me oddly and asked, "Are you hungry?"

6

Shocked by his weird question, it took me a second to answer. When I shook my head no, he nodded, turned, and pulled me again, out of the kitchen and into a hallway. We passed the first door on the right, but stopped at the second door. Again, he turned quickly to me. I was prepared this time, and was able to avoid bumping into him.

He looked me up and down. Then, he jerked the shopping bag from my wrist and the purse from my arm. He threw them on the floor behind him and stepped toward me.

My heart raced. This was it. This was where he was going to rape me or beat me or both.

He put a hand on each of my butt cheeks and squeezed. *So this is how it begins*, I thought. But then he removed his hands and placed them on the fronts of my hips, high on my thighs. He squeezed and squished, and I realized what he was doing. He was patting me down.

When he was satisfied that I had nothing in my pockets, he took a step backward. Without breaking eye contact with me, he opened the door to my right, his left. He flicked on the light.

I didn't want to look in that room, but curiosity got the better of me. I quickly looked away from him and into the room. It was a bathroom. Now I looked back at him, confused.

"Go in there. Do what you have to do. Clean up. Then come back out."

Unsure of what was happening, I slowly turned away from him and stepped into the bathroom.

Behind me he said, "Don't waste time looking for something to use as a weapon. There's nothing in there. And don't try to get out the window. It's nailed shut. I'm standing outside this door with my hand on the knob. Don't be stupid."

He shut the door behind me, and I looked around the room. To the right of the door was the sink and cabinet. At the end of the cabinet was the toilet. At the end of the room, on the other side of the toilet, nestled between each of the walls, was the bathtub. Again, it was spotless. He clearly had an obsession with order and neatness. I was happy that if I was going to be held against my will, at least it was in a clean place. Had the house been crawling with cockroaches and germs, I don't know if I could've handled it as well.

I wasn't sure what I was supposed to be doing. I didn't really need to pee, but I wasn't sure what was in store for me so I figured I'd better do it now.

I stepped over to the toilet and unfastened my jeans. I slid them and my panties down my thighs and sat on the toilet, looking around the room again. When the pee finally started flowing, I wondered if all kidnappings went this way.

Looking for the toilet paper, I saw it hanging from a holder on the side of the cabinet beside the toilet. As I reached for it, I noticed that it hung over the top of the roll. And it was folded into a sharp point.

What kind of kidnapper kept such a tidy house and folded the toilet paper into a point? Then again, what kind of kidnapper offered to feed you and let you pee and clean yourself up? This was so bizarre.

I pulled a few squares off the roll and wiped myself, though I briefly considered skipping the wiping process. Perhaps if I left myself nasty down there it would deter a rape.

I stood and pulled up my panties and jeans. I fastened the button and zipped the zipper. I leaned over and flushed the toilet, considering whether I should fold the toilet paper into a point as it had been. Had I been invited over for dinner at a friend's house, I would've. But I'd been abducted at gunpoint. He and his fancy toilet paper points could kiss my ass.

As I washed my hands, I thought of a way out. I looked at the window above the bathtub and wondered if it was really nailed shut or if it was just something he said to keep me from checking. After I'd dried my hands on the towel that hung perfectly on the towel bar beside the sink, I quickly went to the bathtub. I quietly stepped into the tub and checked the window. It was small, but if I could get it open, I could wiggle through.

I placed my fingers on the window and pushed upward with all my strength. It didn't budge. Damn. Apparently, he was just as honest as he was orderly.

I stepped out of the tub and quickly checked in the cabinet under the sink. There was a pack of toilet paper, a toilet bowl brush standing in a holder, and an extra bottle of liquid antibacterial hand soap. That was it.

He wasn't kidding when he'd said there was nothing in here.

Quickly, I checked the four drawers that stood in a column down one side of the cabinet. A few towels, a few wash cloths, but nothing more.

I opened the cabinet again and took out the white plastic toilet bowl brush. I stood there holding it, wondering if there was anything at all that could be done with it to help me out of this mess. Had any damage ever been caused to anything other than scum by a toilet brush? I doubted it. But it was all I had unless I thought I could squirt the liquid soap hard enough and fast enough to inflict serious eye damage, and I doubted that was possible. In fact, I doubted that even if I could pump it with the speed and strength of a super hero it would reach more than a foot at most. It was useless against every-thing except bacteria and germs.

I swung the toilet brush through the air, trying to judge whether it would hurt him.

Then, the door opened.

# 2

I stood there holding the toilet brush like an idiot, and he stood in the doorway looking at me as if I were an idiot.

"What are you doing with that?" he asked.

"Looking at it."

"Well, put it back and come on."

I returned the brush to the holder under the sink, closed the cabinet door, and left the room.

He flicked off the light behind me and again grabbed my arm. He led me back toward the kitchen.

"You should eat something," he said. He led me to the kitchen table, pulled out a chair, and shoved me down on it. "Sit there."

"Is that what you wanted me to do? I didn't get that from being forced onto the chair," I said sarcastically. Asshole.

From his back pocket, he produced a set of handcuffs. He quickly snapped one around my right wrist. He bent over and snapped the other one under the table. When he walked away, I felt around and found the metal hook he'd attached to the table, apparently for just such a purpose as handcuffing me to it. It was deep. I couldn't twist it, couldn't make it move at all.

Some people had kitchen tables that were made out of pressed sawdust. They often looked as good as those made out of real wood, but they didn't stand up to the same abuse. The cheaper tables scratched and broke easily, which would've been perfect for my situation. At least for me. But this guy wasn't the pressed sawdust type. His table was made of real wood. Heavy. Hardy. Impossible to break and just as impossible to unscrew the hook that tethered me in place.

I tried the handcuffs. They were locked tight around my wrist, so I couldn't pull my hand free, though it didn't stop me from trying.

When I saw it was no use to keep hurting my wrist, I thought maybe I could move the table. I placed both my hands flat against the bottom and lifted. I managed to get it a couple of inches off the floor on my side, but it was too big and heavy to move more than that. Besides, even if I could move it, what was I going to do—slip quietly out of the kitchen while connected to a huge wooden table, walk through the garage and out into the street, totally unnoticed?

"You've got a smart mouth on you," he said as he pulled food from the refrigerator. "Do you talk to everyone like that?"

"No. Just assholes that kidnap me from the mall," I said, again trying to pull my wrist out of the cuff.

With his back to me, he chuckled.

"What the hell is so funny?"

"That you think I'm an asshole."

"Yeah, well, I think it's funny that you think you're not."

"A lot of people think I'm not," he said lightly.

"I doubt that."

"It's true. Everybody I've ever worked with liked me."

"Yeah, well, people in insane asylums aren't the best judges of character."

Again, he chuckled. "I've never worked in an asylum. Although, I believe that would make for interesting work."

"I bet you do," I muttered under my breath. My wrist was burning, but I couldn't keep myself from trying to pull free.

"Do you like mayonnaise on your sandwich?" he asked with his back to me.

11

"What are you serving? Asshole sandwiches? I can't imagine you'd know how to make anything else."

"Mayonnaise it is," he said.

Putting things back in the refrigerator, he said, "You're a little firecracker, aren't you?"

"If by firecracker you mean pissed off woman, then yes. I am."

He chuckled again. "I like that. Keeps things interesting." He carried two sandwiches to the table. He set one in front of me and carried the other with him to the other side of the table where he sat facing me.

Tired of messing around with him, I asked, "Why am I here?"

He smiled. "Because I want you to be."

"That's a bullshit answer."

"Is it?"

"Yeah. Why do you get what you want? I don't want to be here, so give me what I want and let me go."

"I can't do that. You're research to me and I need you."

"What kind of research? Like experiments and stuff?" All kinds of horrible images flashed through my mind. I was terrified of mad—or even slightly angry—scientists experimenting on me, and now he tells me I'm research.

Shit.

He smiled broadly. "No. Not like that."

I stared at him, waiting for him to elaborate but he didn't. Instead, he said, "I'm waiting on you to eat your sandwich. It would be rude for me to eat before you, so if you would be so kind as to take a bite, I'd appreciate it. I'm quite hungry."

"No," I said defiantly to him. "You can starve."

He chuckled. "I said it would be rude. I didn't say it was impossible." He took a bite and chewed slowly.

Defeated, I could only watch.

Seeing me watching him eat, he said, "Eat it. Asshole sandwiches are good." Had I not been handcuffed to his table after he'd abducted me, I might've found that funny.

I looked at my sandwich. It did look good, and I had skipped lunch. I'd planned to stop and grab a burger after the mall and before the salon, but I never made it that far.

Instinctively, I brought up my right hand to grab the sandwich, but it jerked to a stop before it even reached the top of the table. I quickly looked at him, and then used my left hand to awkwardly pick up the sandwich. Taking the first bite, I realized how good it was. The man kept a tidy house and made a mean sandwich. But he was still an asshole.

"Would you like something to drink?"

"What do you have? Piss and vinegar?"

"I'm out of vinegar, but I could whip up a batch of piss if you'd like."

With a deadly serious expression and tone, I said, "You're funny."

"Thanks. I have water, milk, tea, and I think there are some sodas."

"I'll have water."

"Interesting."

"What?"

"I would've thought you'd have taken something more complex. Instead, you chose the simplest of the things I offered."

I didn't respond. Instead, I took another bite of sandwich as he grabbed a bottle of water from the refrigerator. He opened it and set it on the table in front of me.

Returning to his seat, he asked, "You like it?"

"I'd like it more if I were somewhere else eating something else with someone else."

He nodded. "It's going to be fun having you here. You're so unlike the others."

There were so many things wrong with that sentence, I didn't even know where to begin. First of all, it sounded like he planned to keep me around for a while. I suppose it was good that he didn't plan to kill me. At least not yet. But I didn't want to be here. And for him to compare me to 'the others' frightened me. How many others had there been?

He must've seen the look on my face. "Don't worry. I'll take care of you." He leaned forward over the table and added with a smile, "I like you."

Somehow, that didn't make me feel better.

\*\*\*

"Would you like to play a game of Gin Rummy?" he asked after we'd finished eating.

"Yeah. At home. Without you."

"How about here, now, with me? You're going to be here a while, so you might as well get used to the idea and have a little fun. I'm really not such a bad guy." He stood and walked across the room to a drawer, from which he produced a deck of playing cards. He returned to the table, sat, opened the box and began to shuffle the cards.

"How long do you think I'm going to be here?" I asked. "You certainly seem to have some sort of plan."

He shrugged. "You'll be here as long it takes."

"As long as what takes?"

"As long as it takes for me to do my research." He began dealing the cards.

I sighed in frustration. I wasn't getting much from him and it was pissing me off. I needed answers.

He had already picked up his cards and organized them. With his elbow on the table and the cards fanned in his hand, he looked at me. "Are you going to pick up your cards and play with me?"

"Why would I want to play with you? Why would I want to do anything with you? You brought me here against my will and hand-cuffed me to your table. What makes you think I'm even in the mood to play?"

"It's true that I brought you here against your will, but you have to admit that I've been nothing but nice to you. Isn't that right?" He waited patiently for me to answer.

Though I hated to admit it, he was right. I nodded.

"So the question is why wouldn't you want to play with me? Am I not good company?"

He actually had been decent to me so far. But who knew what lay ahead? I was still being held against my will in his house. I really didn't know what to think. Even if I did know what to think, I doubted that I could've thought it because my head was spinning.

I picked up the cards in my left hand and brought them down to my lap, placing them in my right hand. I straightened them out and arranged them. This was the weirdest thing that had ever happened to me. It even trumped the time at the supermarket when someone's kid tripped and fell, grabbing my elastic-waisted Capri pants on the way down. I'd stood there in the crowded store, arms loaded with bags, while my pants slid to my ankles. And that wasn't even the weird part. The weird part came when some guy behind me bent down, grabbed my pants, and pulled them up. Then patted my ass. Compared to this, that was nothing.

As we played, I had questions I needed answered and I wasn't going to let him weasel out of answering them.

"What's your name?" I asked.

"Why do you want to know?"

"So I'll know what to call you."

"Well, it would be nice to hear you call me something other than asshole." He smiled at me over his cards. "My name is Ron."

I waited for him to ask my name, but he didn't. "Don't you want to know my name?"

"I know your name, Nicole."

"How do you know that?"

"Are you surprised?"

"A little."

He chuckled. "It's nothing spectacular, though it would be nice to be able to shock and awe you with some fabulous story of how I studied you for quite some time, took notes of your movements, did a historical report on your family and such. But I'm afraid it's much simpler than that. I looked in your wallet while you were in the bathroom. I saw your name plastered throughout the contents of the purse. It's on your checks, your credit cards, and your driver's license."

I relaxed a little knowing that he hadn't been following me and planning this. I mean, I knew he had planned to kidnap someone; it was just a relief to know it was happenstance that it ended up being me.

"Did you think I'd been stalking you? Hunting you perhaps?"

I shrugged. "I didn't know. You're a psychopath and I can't guess what you do in your spare time."

"A psychopath? Well, that's a step up from asshole, I suppose." He smiled. "I planned to bring someone home with me today. I wasn't sure who until I saw you."

I watched him pick up some cards from the discard pile, and couldn't help but ask, "What was it about me? I mean, why me?"

15

"Look at you. You're a young adult. A woman in her prime years. You're beautiful. You have gorgeous brown hair, which has always been my preferred color. Your smile is enchanting. Your teeth are bright and straight. Your skin is clear and just the right shade of tan. You're fit. When I brought you here, I had no idea just how much fun you were as a person. So as it turns out, not only do you have the looks, but you also have the personality. You're the whole package."

I watched him sort through his cards as I thought about what he'd said. Clearly, he didn't know how to read a person. He called me a young adult, but I was twenty-eight. My smile was enchanting because I had a dentist who worked magic with teeth whitener and veneers. My skin was the right shade of tan because my best friend owned a salon and was an expert at spray tans. Had her salon not also contained a gym, I wouldn't be fit either. And as for my personality, well, I couldn't argue with him there.

Continuing both the game and the interrogation, I asked, "So what do you do, Ron, since you don't work at an asylum?"

He smiled. "Don't you recognize me?"

I looked at him, studying his face. "You mean from the Wanted posters hanging in the Post Office? Sure. I thought you looked familiar."

He laughed. "Your charm just grows on me, Nicole. I thought maybe you would've recognized me from the back of my book."

"What book?"

"I'm not surprised that you don't recognize me. My first novel was the farthest thing from a success. But it's okay, because my next novel, *Held*, is going to be a bestseller."

"You sound pretty confident about that for a guy who failed so miserably the first time," I taunted him. I was aware that it wasn't a good idea to poke the bear, but I couldn't help it. The guy got to me.

"Oh I am certain that the second time will be a success."

"What makes you so sure?"

"Because you're going to help me."

# 3

I didn't know what the hell he was talking about. First he tells me he's a horrible writer, and then he tells me I'm going to help him. I'm not a writer, and I never claimed to be. I didn't know what kind of help I could offer him.

"How could I possibly help you?" I asked, laying down the last card from my hand.

"Well played," he said. We added up our points and he wrote them down on a small notepad in an elegant scrawl. He then shuffled the cards and resumed our conversation. "I mentioned earlier that you were going to help me with my research."

"Yeah, you said that, but you never explained it."

As he dealt, he said, "I need someone to study while I write the book."

"What do you mean, study?" I was as lost now as I was five minutes ago.

He rested his hands on the table and thought of a better way to phrase his words. "The book is about a girl who's held captive, and I'm going to hold you captive until I'm done writing it. That way, I can base what I write on real experiences. I will base my character on you. If you cry, the character will cry. If you scream, the character screams. Make sense now?"

I shuddered at the thought of the things he would do to me just to gauge my response. "That sounds ridiculous."

He sat back and looked as though I'd slapped him. "What do you mean it sounds ridiculous?" He looked as if the word tasted bad in his mouth. His face scrunched up as he said it.

"I mean it sounds stupid. No one wants to read something like that even if you could write it well, which based on the sales of your last book, you can't. It's never going to work."

He pounded his fist on the table, knocking a couple of his cards to the floor. His eyes were wide with anger. His nostrils flared. His chest heaved with each breath.

Quickly, I thought of a way to calm him. I didn't like him when he was calm, but I certainly didn't like him when he was angry.

"But then again, Ron, with me here to add the realism that you need, you might just pull it off. Who knows?"

This seemed to satisfy him. It took a full minute for him to calm down and regain his composure. He picked up his cards from the floor and set about arranging them in his hand.

"I'm sorry," he said.

I didn't know what to say, so I said nothing.

We played that hand in silence. I won again, and he wrote down our scores. As he shuffled the cards, I wondered if my husband had begun to worry yet. Looking at my watch, I saw that it was almost four o'clock. I'd been gone from home since eleven thirty, and had been officially missing since one o'clock. It was nearly dinner time, and I never failed to be home for dinner with my husband and son. If he hadn't started worrying yet, he soon would.

"Sometimes I get...angry." After a moment, he added, "I don't suppose there's a need to apologize. After all, you'll learn soon enough about my anger."

"What does that mean?" I was afraid it meant he was going to take his anger out on me.

"Don't worry about it," he said. "Let's just play. No need to ruin a perfectly good afternoon with talk of anger. Now what do you like to do in your spare time?"

I opened my mouth to smart off to him, but before I could a clatter came from the hallway. Ron jumped up from his chair, and I spun around. I didn't know what had caused the sound, but I had a feeling he did.

At first I saw nothing because there was nothing to see. But then the first door on the right in the hallway burst open, and what emerged was beyond my imagination.

It was a woman, I could tell that much because she was naked. But I couldn't have given her description to the police because she was covered in blood and filth. Her hair was long and stringy and caked with both wet and dry dirt. Her eyes were wide, and even from this distance, I could see the fear. And I could smell her. It was a combination of body odor, fecal matter, and piss.

I wasn't sure whether or not she saw me, but I knew she saw Ron. When her eyes found him, she screamed. Then, she turned and ran into what I assumed was the living room. Ron bolted after her. I listened to the sounds coming from the next room, trying to figure out what the hell was going on.

Something crashed to the floor—probably a lamp—and then there were sounds that could only be Ron hitting her. Some carried the smacking sound of slaps, while others had the heavy tone of a punch. She yelled and screamed. He told her to shut up.

Then, Ron came backing out of the living room, dragging the woman by her hair as she kicked and screamed. She tried to remove his hands from her head, tried to scratch him, tried to hit him, but she succeeded only in making him angry.

He slammed her head to the floor and pivoted on his left foot. He sat on her belly, one leg on each side of her. As she continued to kick and scream and thrash around, trying to get in some good blows, Ron got in a few of his own, punching and slapping her repeatedly in the face. At one point, he choked her.

No longer able to stomach the sight of her being beaten, I looked away.

When the slapping stopped, I looked back and saw Ron dragging her limp body through the open doorway, back to where she'd been.

I was left sitting in the kitchen wondering who she was and what was going on.

Suddenly, everything was real. I was being held in a house with a madman who had been torturing a woman for no telling how long. I didn't dare ponder how long she might've been here or what sort of horrors she'd been subjected to.

Ron had two sides to him of which I was now aware. He had a calm side, which allowed him to seem friendly and normal. Then, he had a dark side, full of simmering rage that was ready to explode at any moment.

He was capable of anything.

I was scared for my life. Fearing I'd never see my husband and son again, I pulled on my hand, willing the damn thing to slide out of the handcuff. I put my left hand on the chain between the cuffs and pulled. I even put my feet on the edge of the table and pushed against it as I pulled. This resulted in nothing but pain.

On the verge of tears, I put my feet back on the floor. This couldn't be happening to me. Not to me.

Minutes later, Ron walked back into the kitchen. He washed his hands and returned to his seat at the table. He sat there for a while looking at his cards, which lay face-down on the table. Finally, he picked them up and looked at me as though nothing had happened.

"Whose turn is it?" he asked.

Puzzled beyond belief, I stuttered, "Yours, I think."

He smiled at me and drew a card from the pile.

For a few minutes, I played cards with him, considering asking about the woman. I realized he could easily turn the same anger on me that he'd turned on her. I didn't want to be on the receiving end of his fists. But I had to know.

"Ron, can I ask you something?"

He looked up at me and smiled. "You just did."

Ignoring my hatred for people who say things like that, I asked, "Who was that woman?"

"Stephanie."

Seeing that he wasn't going to offer anything else, I pushed him. "What's her story?"

Picking up cards from the discard pile, he said, "Stephanie is a woman I met one night in a bar. She wanted to come home with me, so she did. I think she's changed her mind about wanting to be here, though. She doesn't seem happy."

"Where is she? What's in that room?"

20

"That's the basement. She's been down there since the first night. She doesn't like it down there, but she doesn't have a choice."

"Why don't you let her go?"

He jerked his head toward me, and for a second, I saw the angry Ron.

I quickly softened the question with, "I mean, why keep her around?"

His face relaxed. "I have needs and urges. She helps me with those. But did you see her? I'm afraid she's just about fulfilled her purpose. She's far too thin and on the verge of madness, I believe."

"Are you going to let her go?" I asked as I drew a card.

"Of course not. I can't do that. You're a smart girl, Nicole. You know I can't let her go. She'll alert the authorities. Then what? They arrest me, I go to prison, and my novel will never be written. I can't let that happen."

"So what—you're going to kill her?" I hated saying the words. I knew that saying it wouldn't be putting the thought in his head. He already knew what he was going to do, but it still felt like I was giving him the idea.

"Do you have a better suggestion?"

I shook my head and fell silent for a while. Afraid to know the answer but more afraid not to, I asked, "Do you plan to kill me, Ron?" I hated the crack in my voice when I spoke. It betrayed my brave persona.

For such a long time, he didn't answer. I began to think his silence meant that yes, he did plan to kill me. But finally, he spoke. "I don't know what I'll do with you yet, to be honest. You seem to think I have some master plan, but I don't. All I have is an idea for a great story and high hopes. But with you, this idea will flourish and turn into a wonderful reality. When that happens, who knows what will become of you. I guess in the end, it will depend on you. There. I finally beat you a hand," he said as he laid his last card on top of the discard pile.

He tallied his score while I tallied mine, though I had to count my cards twice. I was having trouble concentrating. Something about having my life hanging in the balance and an uncertain future had me rattled.

After writing the scores on the notepad and adding them up, Ron announced that I'd won. He congratulated me, and suggested we play another game. I protested.

"What else are you going to do if not play cards with me?" he asked.

It was a good question. I shrugged and he shuffled the cards.

"So tell me about yourself. I know so very little about you," he said. "I'm dying to know more. In fact, I want to know everything."

"I don't think so."

"Come on. If I'm to base a character on you, shouldn't I know every detail about you and your life?"

"I thought you were just going to use my responses in your book. You didn't say that you were modeling a character off me. That's different."

"Does it matter? You don't exactly have a choice in the matter, do you?"

He was right. I didn't. But I still didn't want him knowing everything about me.

"How about I pour us a drink and you tell me about yourself, starting at the beginning. Would you like a drink?" he asked as he got up and went to a cabinet.

I opened my mouth to say no, but decided this was probably the perfect time to drink. My nerves were frayed, and I was on edge. Just one drink wouldn't hurt. So instead of declining, I asked if he had orange juice and Vodka. Fortunately, he did. He made us each a drink and returned to the table.

I took a sip of mine and realized that in addition to being an immaculate housekeeper and maker of awesome sandwiches, he could easily serve drinks in any club. Daytime Bartender Moonlights as Madman. Now there's a novel.

"Where were you born?" he asked, kicking off the interview.

"Poplar Bluff."

"Is that where you grew up?"

"No."

"Where'd you grow up?"

"A small town about an hour away from there."

"Did you live with your mother and father?"

"Yes."

"Do you have brothers or sisters?"

22

"One brother."

"Where does he live?"

"He doesn't."

"What does that mean?"

"He died in a car accident three weeks after graduating from high school."

He studied my face, probably making mental notes of my reaction and my emotions. Then, he continued with his barrage of questions. "Were you two close?"

"Yes."

"Did your parents fight a lot?"

"No."

"No? That's rare these days, isn't it?"

I shrugged. "They fought some, but no more than anybody else."

"So your childhood was a happy one?"

"Yeah, I guess it was."

"Were you molested by anyone?"

"I think that's enough. There's no sense in this."

"Just answer the question. I'm just trying to get a feel of what your life was like and what made you the person you are today."

I sighed. "No, I wasn't molested, I wasn't beaten, and I wasn't raped by anyone in or out of my family."

He nodded. "How old were you when you first had sex?"

"Come on. This is ridiculous."

"It's not ridiculous. It's research."

"Why would you ever have to know that?"

"For the book, of course."

"My ass. There's no reason you need to know that. And even if you did, you can make it up. It's a fiction book, not a biography of my life."

"It's all part of your makeup, part of why you are the wonderful person you are now. I like to know how things come to be what they are. Don't you want to know things like that?"

I certainly wanted to know what made him the way he was. Then again, maybe I didn't.

"I'll answer your questions only if you swear that you'll answer any questions I may have now or in the future." I stared at him as he agreed, trying to determine whether or not he was being honest. Of course he was. Apparently the one thing he didn't do is lie.

"I swear to you I will always be honest and answer any questions you may have. I haven't lied to you as of yet, and I have no plans to do so. You may ask me anything you like, but I do hope you hold off until I've asked all my questions of you."

"Fine."

"Fine," he agreed.

I took a long drink before answering. "I was sixteen."

"Your boyfriend?"

"Yes."

"Did you love him?"

"I thought I did. But at sixteen, nobody knows what real love is."

"I take it he isn't your husband."

It was my turn to chuckle. "No."

"Why is that amusing to you?"

"Because he and my husband are completely different. They have no similarities whatsoever."

He laid down his last card and we began to add our scores. After jotting them on the notepad, he shuffled the cards again. "Were you a good student?"

"Yes."

"You made good grades?"

"Yes. In fact, I rarely had homework, I never studied, and yet I was an A student."

"So learning came naturally for you?"

"I guess so," I said and finished my drink.

After shuffling the cards, he set them on the table and got up. He took my empty glass to the counter and refilled it. As soon as he brought it back, I took a drink.

He sat in his chair, scooted it up to the table, and asked, "Were you promiscuous as a teenager?"

"No," I said, taking a little offense to such a question.

"Are you promiscuous now?"

"No," I snapped. "I'm married."

"There are a lot of promiscuous women who are married." He pointed to the hallway and said, "She's married, but that didn't stop her from offering herself to me in the bar that night."

24

I swallowed the fear and the lump in my throat. He had held her here all this time knowing that she had a family. The man had no sympathy.

"Yeah, well I'm happily married, and I don't do stuff like that."

He nodded. "Good. You shouldn't."

"You're going to give me a lecture on things I shouldn't do?"

"You find that odd?"

"Yeah. You kidnap people, hold them here for no telling how long, do no telling what to them, but your morals are intact enough to know that I shouldn't sleep around? That's crazy."

"You think I'm crazy?"

"I said that's crazy, but now that you mention it, yeah. I think maybe I should count these cards because clearly you're not playing with a full deck."

He threw his cards on the table and stood up so fast his chair toppled over backward onto the floor, making a noise loud enough to cause me to nearly jump out of my skin.

He began to pace back and forth across the room. He started off mumbling something to himself, but then he talked louder. So loud, in fact, his voice boomed, echoing off the walls. He alternated between waving his arms around and placing his hands on his hips.

"I am nothing but nice to you, and yet you call me crazy. I bring you into my home and treat you well, and yet you call me crazy. I could've taken you straight to the basement and locked you down there, but I didn't. And yet you call me crazy." He walked quickly over to me and leaned down, his face only inches from mine. "I can show you crazy. You haven't seen crazy. Would you like to see crazy, Nicole?"

This guy was nuttier than a squirrel turd, but it was obvious that he didn't think so. It brought to mind a book I read once called *Annie's Revenge*. The author stated many times that insane people never doubt their sanity. I guess she was right. Crazy people don't know they're crazy.

Quickly, I thought of a way out of this situation. I hadn't failed to notice he'd mentioned locking me in the basement with what's-her-name. I didn't know what all was down there or what went on, but I'd seen her and knew I wanted no part of it. So I had to do something, anything, to keep myself from experiencing her fate.

25

"Look, Ron, I'm sorry. I didn't mean that you're crazy. It's just that I felt like you were insinuating that I slept around, and it made me angry. I was just lashing out." I surprised myself with how calm I was being. Inside, I was shaking like a Chihuahua in a snow storm. But outside, I was so cool cucumbers were jealous.

Ron stood up and put his hands on his hips. He stood there looking down at me for a minute. Then, he smiled.

"That's why I like you. You're full of fire, but you know when you've crossed a line. None of the others ever had sense enough to know that." He reached out and placed his hand on my head. I wanted to pull away, but knew that it wouldn't be wise to do so. Even as he slid his hand down the back of my head and neck, I didn't move a muscle.

Consulting his watch, he said, "I'm afraid I didn't learn all I wanted to learn about you, but it's getting late. I have many things to do before going to bed. But I suppose there'll be plenty of time to learn all I want about you, won't there?"

I nodded, fighting back tears.

He crossed his left arm over his chest and brought his right arm up, placing his thumb under his chin and his index finger over his lips. Clearly, he was thinking. I was afraid to even imagine what was on his sick mind.

As if he could read my mind, he said aloud, "I'm thinking that maybe you should stay up here with me." He looked at me to judge my reaction, but there wasn't one. I didn't know where I'd rather be, other than home.

"Yes, the basement is a nasty place, and I like you too much to put you down there. So far, anyway." He smiled. I didn't.

He unlocked the cuff from the kitchen table, but not from my wrist. He held it tightly and pulled me up. Holding my shackled wrist in one hand, he put his other arm around me, squeezing my shoulder slightly as he led me down the hallway.

"You know, if you let me go right now, I'll never tell."

"Now you and I both know that's not true, Nicole. That's the very first thing you would do."

We kept walking down the hallway, past the basement door, past the bathroom door. At the end of the hall, there was a door on each side. We stopped and waited while he thought aloud again.

"Let's see. Would you like to sleep with me or alone?"

"Alone," I said quickly. The thought of sleeping with him sent a chill down my spine and a ripple through my stomach.

"Yes, I suppose for now you may sleep alone. But it won't always be that way," he said before kissing the top of my head. If I threw up now, my heart would surely come up with the sandwich and the vodka because it had beaten its way right out of its place in my chest. It felt like it was flapping around in circles. I did my best to show no fear.

"Come on then," he said as he led me through the door on the left. This left me assuming that the door on the right was the door to his bedroom. I fought to keep away the images of what his room must be like.

He turned on the light, and I looked around the room. There were two windows, one on the end wall and another on the back wall. Both were covered with blinds and heavy drapes so I couldn't see out and no one could see in.

The walls were beige, the ceiling was white, and the trim around the windows, doors, floor and ceiling was white. On the floor was a cream-colored carpet.

The bed looked to be a queen size with a metal headboard and footboard that resembled a wrought iron fence. On the bed was a burgundy comforter with matching pillow shams and a lot of pillows. On each side of the bed was a nightstand. On each of those nightstands stood a black lamp with a beige shade.

Across the room was a large armoire. On the wall opposite the bed was a dresser, over which hung a large mirror. Other than a few paintings that hung on the walls, that was it. It was a simple, beautiful room. The man was a sadistic psycho, but he was one hell of a decorator and housekeeper.

As was the case in all the other rooms, there wasn't a speck of dust or dirt to be seen, which made the woman in the basement an even bigger mystery. She'd been filthy, so unlike everything else I'd seen so far.

Ron led me into the room and over to the bed. He spun me around to face him. With the bed touching the back of my legs and him standing only inches in front of me, I instinctively began to panic like the caged animal I was.

Still holding my shackled wrist in his hand, he said, "You're not going to like this, I'm sure. But it has to be done. Take off your shoes," he ordered.

Without breaking eye contact, I put the toes of my left foot on the heel of my right and pushed off the shoe. I repeated the process for the other shoe while he watched and my heart raced.

"Now would you like to unfasten your jeans or would you like me to?"

"Why do they need to be unfastened at all?"

"You can't sleep in your clothes." He smiled.

"Yeah, I can. Let's do that."

"No, let's not. Take them off. It's not becoming for a woman to sleep in her clothes. Besides, wouldn't you be more comfortable without the restrictions of your clothes? Without the tight fabric stretched taut across your delicate skin?" He ran his fingers down my side as he spoke, and I don't think I just imagined the lusty tone in his voice.

"No, I think I'm good with leaving them on."

"Take them off, or I will take them off," he barked.

His shouting scared me. Against all my judgment, I unbuttoned my jeans. Not wanting to see the angry side of him, I unzipped them and pushed them down to my ankles. Still holding my wrist, he bent over with me as I pulled the jeans off my feet. When I stood, I still had hopes that he wouldn't order me to take off anything else. I was wrong, and not for the first time that day.

"Take off your shirt."

"I don't see why—"

"Take it off," he barked again. His voice, when raised to that level, was very painful on the ears. The bass in his tone rattled my chest and plucked at my already frayed nerves.

I pulled my left arm out of the sleeve. He let go of my right wrist long enough for me to pull my arm through the sleeve, then he cupped it back in his big hand. I pulled the t-shirt over my head and held it in front of my chest.

He pulled the shirt away from me and laid it on the nightstand. "Now the bra."

I thought about protesting, but if the third time really was the charm, then it would be a stupid thing to do. So I reached behind me with my left hand and popped the clasp on the bra. I slid my arms out while he watched. He took the bra from me as soon as I was free of it, tossing it on the table with my shirt.

He leaned back and stared at my nearly naked body, which I tried to cover with the one free arm I had.

"You shouldn't try to hide yourself. You have a wonderful body. You should be proud of it."

"You were just saying that I shouldn't be promiscuous." I reminded him. I said it lightly and quietly, hoping that if said in the proper tone it wouldn't send him into a rage.

"That's why I like you so much. You keep me on my toes," he said and leaned into me.

I stood there, naked except for my socks and panties, as he gently kissed my neck. Had he been my boyfriend or husband, this would've been nice. But he was a madman who'd kidnapped me, and it was horrible.

Over and over, he kissed me softly on the neck, still holding my right wrist in his left hand. I wanted to cry, but was sure that if I did, he'd show his angry side again. So I bit my lip and held it back. When I felt him cup my left breast, I nearly lost it. But somehow I managed to keep it together.

After a few minutes of kissing and fondling, he pulled away from me slowly and smiled.

"Time for bed." He reached behind me and pulled back the comforter. I felt him tossing pillows out of the way.

I was frozen. All I could think about was how horrifying it would be to have his large body atop me, raping me. I was too scared to move.

"Come on," he said. "Get into bed. I've got a lot of things to do."

He pushed me backward, and I fell onto the bed. Amazingly, he still held my wrist. He turned me around so that my head was on the pillows. Then, he got up on his knees beside me on the bed.

My heart raced. This was it.

He pulled my arms up over my head and wound the handcuff behind a bar of the headboard and clamped it around my other wrist. I was shackled to the bed now.

With my arms held above my head by the cuffs, he didn't have to hold onto my wrist. He sat up on his knees and drank me in with his eyes. When he leaned down toward me, I nearly screamed. As he kissed each of my breasts, I squeezed my eyes shut and pretended I was anywhere but here.

The movements of him getting off the bed made me open my eyes. I was afraid that I would find him standing beside the bed undressing. Instead, I found him walking to the end of the bed where he pulled off each of my socks. He then pulled the comforter up over my body, covering my exposed breasts.

Seeing that rape wasn't on his agenda for this evening, I relaxed a little. I was sure that at some point, he was going to have me, but it didn't look like it was going to be tonight.

"Sleep tight, Nicole."

He smiled and turned, flicking off the light before leaving the room. He left the door open, which I didn't care for at all. I would've preferred it closed, so as to have some sort of warning if he sneaked into the room in the middle of the night.

Alone now, I saw no reason to keep holding back my tears and my panic, so I let loose. I cried silently so as to not alert him, but I cried hard and long. I was crying when I heard him walk down the steps to the basement, and an eternity later when I heard him coming back up the steps, I was still crying.

The tears weren't just for me. They weren't tears of self-pity. At least not all of them. They were tears for my husband, Wade, and for my son, Mason. Mason was only one year old. One year and one month. He wouldn't even remember me if I never came back. Wade would have to teach him about me from photographs and stories. It made me sad to think that I might not be there for all of his firsts. His first day of school, losing his first tooth, his first girlfriend, it all made me sad.

And Wade. How long would he grieve for me? How long would he wait before he went on to find someone else? Would he pick someone like me? Would she love him and Mason as much as I did?

I cried myself to sleep that night, and it was to be the first of many nights like it.

# 4

When I woke the next morning, I was startled by Ron's presence. He stood at the side of the bed, hands in the pockets of his khaki slacks, staring at me with a smile on his face. It was creepy.

"Good morning," he said. "I trust that you slept well."

I tried to rub the sleep from my eyes, but of course I couldn't. My hands were handcuffed, my arms still bound above my head. My shoulders ached, and though I tried wiggling my fingers, I couldn't feel them.

"Here, let me help you." He placed a knee on the bed and leaned over, removing the handcuffs from my wrists and bringing my arms down to my sides.

The pain was sharp and sudden, and it made me gasp. My shoulders were sore, the muscles stiff from being in that position all night.

"Do you need a moment?" he asked.

With my arms at my sides, I nodded. Moments later, as the blood began to circulate through my arms and hands, the tingling started. It was a painful feeling, as if millions of needles were poking into my skin over and over.

I tried not to show that it hurt, but I winced and gasped more than once, giving me away.

"I'm sorry about that. I would like very much if I didn't have to restrain you, but I'm afraid I can't trust you. Maybe tonight we can figure out another way that will cause you less pain."

I waited on the tingling to subside, hating the thought of spending another night, another day, or even another second in this house with him. But I saw no way out.

"Okay, let's go," he said, holding my wrist. "Let's get up and shower and get ready for the day."

Slowly, I slid myself to the edge of the bed and stood. I brought my aching arm up and rubbed my eyes as I followed Ron down the hall to the bathroom. He turned on the light and stepped aside, letting me enter.

"I'll leave you alone, but I'm right outside this door. You should have everything you need. If not, let me know." He smiled.

I went into the bathroom and shut the door. Instinctively, I reached for the lock, but there wasn't one. I couldn't lock the door, but at least there was a door between us. At least he didn't stand in the open doorway, leering at me while I did my business.

Looking around, I saw my clothes, folded neatly and stacked on the counter beside the sink. My bra was on top. I picked it up and brought it to my nose. Inhaling deeply, I smelled a laundry detergent that I didn't use. He'd washed my clothes.

Beside the clothes were many personal hygiene items. A towel, a washcloth, a toothbrush, a tube of toothpaste, and a comb.

After peeing, I slipped out of my panties and carried the towel and washcloth to the bathtub. There was no towel bar, so I draped the towel over the shower curtain rod. I stepped into the tub and pulled close the curtain. I looked to the shelf in the corner and saw a new bar of soap and a bottle of shampoo. He'd thought of everything.

I washed thoroughly, making sure to wash twice in all the places where he'd touched and kissed me.

After the shower, I stood in front of the sink putting on my bra and t-shirt. I'd been debating whether or not I wanted to wear my panties again, but then I found a fresh pair in the stack of clothes on the counter. I pulled them on, and then my jeans. Once dressed, I brushed my teeth and combed my hair.

When I opened the door, Ron was standing there, just as he'd said he would be. A madman of his word.

He smiled at me, took my wrist in his hand, and snapped the cuff around it. I followed as he led me to the kitchen and once again hooked the handcuff to the underside of the table.

"I'm sure you're hungry," he said. I watched as he pulled items from the refrigerator and carried them to the counter by the stove. "Do you like scrambled eggs?"

I thought of not answering, but decided I was too hungry to ignore the opportunity to eat. "Yes."

With his back to me, he nodded. "Good. While I cook, I see no reason why we can't continue our conversation from last night, do you?"

I rolled my eyes, knowing that he couldn't see me. "Sure," I said, unenthusiastically.

"Very well. Did you attend college?"

"Yes."

"In what field do you have a degree?"

"I don't have a degree. I didn't finish college."

He glanced back at me over his shoulder. "You didn't finish? Why not?"

"My mom got sick. I had to go home and take care of her. After she died, I wasn't interested in school anymore. I never went back."

"That's a pity. You said you were married. Where did you meet your husband?"

"He was a friend of a friend. I met him at a birthday party."

"How innocent. When was that?"

"Seven years ago."

"Do you love him?"

"Of course. Why would I have married him if I didn't love him?"

"I'm not saying you didn't love him at one time, but many people fall out of love. I was just inquiring as to whether or not you still love him, after seven years."

"Well I do. More now than then, in fact." It pissed me off to have this asshole asking me personal questions, but if it kept him calm, I would suck it up and push through. Besides, I knew there were far worse things he could be doing to me than prying into my personal history.

33

"Do you believe that he loves you as much as you love him?"

"Yes."

"Do you think he's searching for you right now, as we speak?"

I imagined Wade and what he must be going through. I had no doubt that he was devastated. We'd never been apart. I'd never failed to come home, nor had he. We went to bed together every night, and we woke up next to each other every morning. We didn't fight. We didn't argue, though from time to time we did disagree with one another. My heart sank at the thought of how sad he must be.

"Yes, I do."

"Do you think he'll find you?"

I could tell by the way he stopped what he was doing and studied my face that my answer would be pivotal. Quickly but carefully, I weighed my answer. I wasn't sure what to say, but I figured I should say no. Ron thought he was smarter than other people, so if I said my husband would find me, he would be furious, feeling as though I thought he was too dumb to outsmart my husband. He may even move me to another location, one not nearly as nice as this one.

"Probably not," I said.

He smiled and nodded. Having answered the question correctly, I breathed a sigh of relief.

He carried two plates to the table and set one in front of me. The aroma of the eggs and buttered toast made my stomach rumble. He sat across from me, and we began to eat. I didn't have to ask why I was eating my scrambled eggs with a spoon and he had a fork. It was obvious. A fork was a weapon. And though I supposed I could possibly put out one of his eyes with the handle of the spoon if I got really lucky, I knew that wouldn't happen. Even if I did manage to cause him sort of damage with the rounded utensil, I was still handcuffed to the heavy table.

"Is it my turn to ask you questions yet?" I asked after the first bite.

"I suppose that would be fine."

"Where were you born?"

"Milwaukee."

"Is that where you were raised?"

"No. My family moved around a great deal, so we were never in one place for long."

34

"Was your father in the military?"

"No."

"Then why did you move around so much?"

"My father was a criminal and always on the run. Milk?"

"Yes. Did your parents fight a lot?"

He was quiet for a moment as he poured us each a glass of milk. I thought he wasn't going to answer, but as he handed me a glass and returned to his seat, he said, "My father seemed to think of my mother as a punching bag. He beat her more days than not, and never for a good reason. It was always something like her spaghetti was too dry or her hair was out of place."

"Why didn't she leave him?"

"A mother of six? Not likely to happen. She had no way to support so many children, so it was easier for her to endure my father's beatings than try to make it alone in the world with such heavy baggage."

He took a couple of bites without saying another word.

"Did he ever beat you?"

"Yes, many times. He beat each of us. Except the girls. Their punishments were far worse than a beating."

I knew what that meant, so I left it alone.

"Were you a good student?"

"Yes, as good as one can be with a home life such as mine. I studied hard and made good grades. I had no friends, though. I was never in one place long enough to make any."

"Did you go to college?"

"No. I was too busy working to support my family. I barely had enough money for us all to eat, much less waste on college."

"You seem to be educated, though. I mean, you talk better than most people."

He nodded. "Yes, I suppose I do. That's years of hard work and practice. I learned a long time ago that if you want people to take you seriously, you can't walk around looking, acting, and talking like you have no proper upbringing. I may have been raised in a poor, abusive household, but I certainly don't want people to look at me and see it."

I opened my mouth to ask him something else, but a scream stopped the words from forming.

Looking at Ron, I couldn't tell if he'd heard it or not. Surely he had. There was no way he couldn't have. It was loud. It wasn't until he shook his head slowly while staring at his plate that I realized he had heard it.

"Is that the woman in the basement?"

"I'm afraid so."

"Why's she screaming?"

"Because she hasn't learned her lesson yet," he said with a hint of anger. "I've told her many times that I can't have her screaming like that. If the neighbors were to hear her, I could get in a lot of trouble. Yet she insists on screaming. I suppose I shall have to punish her again."

Afraid to know but more afraid not to, I asked, "By punish her, what do you mean?"

He looked up at me and chewed slowly. "Are you sure you want to know? It isn't pleasant, Nicole. I wouldn't think someone as beautiful and innocent as you would be interested in such atrocities."

I wanted to know, but I didn't want him to get angry at me for being something other than what he thought I was. I got the distinct feeling that it would send him into a rage like none I'd seen so far. Besides, I probably didn't want to know.

"You're right. I don't want to know."

He nodded and said, "I thought so. Let's just hope you never have to find out." Seeing the look on my face he added, "When I brought you here, I had every intention of putting you in the basement alongside her. But I so enjoyed your fire that I decided to keep you up here with me. The basement is no place for a woman like you, a woman I adore so much."

"Has she always been down there?"

He nodded. "From the very moment I brought her here. I didn't even want to bring her home with me, you see. She kept insisting on it, so finally, I brought her with me. I knocked her out when I pulled into the garage, and I carried her downstairs. When she woke, she fought a good fight. It excited me, I have to admit. She's got spunk, like you. But her spunk is only to benefit herself. She only wishes to be free. I've tried many times to strike up a conversation with her, such as we're having now, but she'll take no part."

My appetite was fading now, and I ate slower as I listened to him talk.

"I do miss good conversation. It gets so lonely around here with no one to talk to. I have so many ideas and no one to share them with. I'm so glad you're here."

"If you long for companionship, why don't you marry?"

"I was married. To a wonderful woman. But she didn't understand me. She wasn't a very good conversationalist anyway. Not nearly as good as you. She wanted to talk about shopping and hair and clothes. I care nothing for any of those things, and I certainly don't want to waste hours of my day talking about them. Not when there are far more important matters at hand."

The woman in the basement, Stephanie, screamed louder and louder until Ron couldn't take it anymore. He threw his fork onto his plate and stood. As he stomped his way out of the kitchen, threw open the door to the basement, and pounded his way down the steps, I wished there was a way I could warn her that he was coming. Better yet, I wished there was a way I could help her escape.

Moments after the screams abruptly stopped, the doorbell rang.

My heart pounded and I opened my mouth to yell for help. That's when Ron's hand came from behind me and clamped down over my mouth. He whispered into my ear, "If you say one word, I'll kill your husband and child. Do you understand?" Slowly, he took his hand away from my mouth.

"You don't know where I live," I said with the fire he liked so much. "So how can you kill anyone I know?"

He smiled, and in an even voice said, "In your purse is a driver's license. On that license is an address. At that address resides your husband and child." He went through the kitchen and into the living room to answer the door, leaving me at the table where I sat silently until he returned. I would do nothing to jeopardize the welfare of my husband and son. He knew that. This was how he was going to hold me here.

When he returned, I asked, "How do you know I have a child?"

"Seriously, Nicole. You're a smart woman. I find it very unattractive for you to pretend to be dense." He washed his hands at the sink. While drying them on a paper towel, he turned to me. "You really don't know how I know?"

I thought for a second, but I couldn't find a way he could've known.

Tired of waiting for it to come to me, he said, "In your purse is a pacifier. Either you have a bizarre obsession or you have a child. I choose to believe the latter. Am I wrong?"

I shook my head.

"I thought not. I believe I'm right about you, Nicole. We are going to do great things, you and me."

I was afraid of what he meant by that.

# 5

For the next month, my days were filled with the same routine. I was released from the bed, allowed to shower, fed breakfast, and spent the day trapped in conversations and card games. Occasionally, the cards were replaced with board games, but that was the only variance to the routine.

Ron had changed the way he handcuffed me to the bed. My arms were no longer straight above my head. Instead, they were angled outward toward the corners of the headboard. It was better, but every morning, my shoulders and neck were stiff and sore, and they ached for the biggest part of the day. I didn't complain about it. After all, I was being held captive. If that's the worst thing I had to endure, I'd consider myself lucky.

On days when Ron had to leave the house, he handcuffed me to the bed. He put my arms in the usual position, and he even stretched my legs out and handcuffed each ankle to the footboard. He then used a pink bandana to gag me, saying I sure looked pretty in pink. He would stroke my hair and tell me that he hated to leave me like that, but he still couldn't trust me while he was away.

Ron watched my every move. When I asked him about it, he told me he was studying me for the novel he was writing. When I asked how the book was coming along, he said he hadn't started it yet, but was close. I was close too. Close to losing my mind. I was trying to keep it together, hoping that if I could keep him satisfied with conversation and company, he'd write the damn book and let me go. I pushed away any thoughts that said otherwise.

Stephanie continued to scream from time to time in the basement. It always angered Ron, who stomped down there in a huff. Moments later, Stephanie fell silent, and each time, I wondered if he'd killed her. I knew enough about him now to know it was only a matter of time until it happened. As selfish as it was, I couldn't help but wonder what was going to happen to me after he'd killed her. Would I take her place? Would he begin to do the things to me that he apparently enjoyed doing to her? I hoped not. But I just didn't know.

Every night, he undressed me. And every night, as I stood before him naked, he kissed my neck. Once I was strapped to the bed, he kissed and touched my body. Though there had been a couple of times when I was sure it was going to happen, he still hadn't raped me. He would though. It was only a matter of time. I could tell by the way he kissed and touched me when I was naked that he wanted me. Badly. Even if I'd failed to notice the lust in his touch, I couldn't fail to notice the bulge in his khaki slacks. I wasn't sure how long he'd hold out before giving in to his desires.

During the second week, he noticed my leg hair had grown to be stubbly and said we were going to have to do something about it. Personally, I wanted the hair to grow as long the hair on my head if it meant it would turn him off to me physically, but he insisted we get rid of it. Of course, he wouldn't buy a razor and let me shave my own legs. And it was a good thing for him that he didn't. I would've disassembled that sucker and went to slicing and dicing on him in a hurry. He bought an electric shaver and shaved my legs with it. It was humiliating, but again, if this was as bad as it got, then fine by me.

The third week, I had my period. He bought the tampons I asked for. In fact, anything I needed, he provided without so much as a complaint. Had he not been a psychopath, he would've made an excellent husband.

40

The fourth Wednesday into my captivity, things went wrong. Horribly wrong.

I'd been living up to my end of this arrangement with my smart mouth. He liked the way I handled myself. I had a feeling it was what kept me out of the basement. His moods changed quicker than the flicker of a light bulb, though. One second, I was mouthing off to him and he was laughing and loving it. The next second, he was showing his angry side because of something I'd said. I wasn't used to dealing with schizophrenic psychopaths and wasn't sure how to handle it. I thought I was doing a pretty good job, though, for someone thrust into a situation like this.

I was cuffed to the kitchen table while Ron prepared dinner. With his back to me, he mentioned his plans for the evening.

"I believe it's time, Nicole."

"Time for what?"

"It's time for me to show you how I feel about you."

I looked down at my cuffed wrist with the chafed skin. "I think I know how you feel about me, Ron."

"I don't think you do. And even if you did, I believe it's time I showed you."

My mind spun as I tried to think of what he could possibly mean. Several things popped into my mind, but I prayed for each one to be wrong.

"Are you going to let me go now?" I asked, knowing the answer would be no.

He chuckled. "No. Tonight, I will come to you."

"What does that mean?"

"It means I will come to you, Nicole. I will come to your bed, and you will have me."

"You come to my bed and I'll have you, alright. I'll have you arrested."

He threw his head up toward the ceiling and laughed a deep laugh. I watched as he continued to laugh, shaking his head with amusement.

"Oh, Nicole. I'm so glad you're here. This last month has been such a joy for me. You have no idea how good you've been for me and how much I've enjoyed having you here. That's one reason I plan to come to you tonight. I'd like to show you how much I appreciate you."

41

"No, I'm okay."

I watched him tense. "What do you mean you're okay?"

"I have some idea of how much you appreciate me. There's no need to show me." I tried to say it lightly, hoping to avoid making him angry. I knew immediately that it hadn't worked.

He spun around to face me. "I'm going to show you. I've been more than good to you, and what have I asked in return? Nothing. I've asked nothing of you. I provide you with food, a proper place to sleep, all the things you need, and I have asked nothing in return." His cheeks grew red with anger, and even from across the room I saw his nostrils flare.

"Hey," I yelled, all my restraint falling away. "You make it sound like I asked to move in here with you. You kidnapped me! To say that you provide me with food and a proper place to sleep is stupid. You brought me here against my will. You've asked nothing of me? You've asked everything of me! You asked me to be compliant and submissive. To not scream so people can hear. You've asked me to assist you in writing a book that no one will read. You want me to keep you in conversation and be good company for you. And now you ask me to let you have your way with me. I don't want to be here, asshole, but I'm stuck. I've made this easy on you so far." Before I could go on, he laughed a loud, fake laugh.

"You've made this easy on me so far?" He laughed again. It wasn't his normal you're-so-funny-and-cute-and-that's-why-I-keep-you-out-of-the-basement laugh. This was thin and strained. The man was cracking up in front of me. Suddenly, the laughter stopped and he glared at me.

A chill ran down my spine. I wasn't a fortune teller or a psychic, but I could see that I'd just screwed up.

He turned his back to me and continued making dinner in silence. I welcomed the quiet, but it worried me. I'd clearly made him angry. This quiet anger was new, a side he hadn't shown until now.

With neither of us saying a word, we ate.

Usually, we played cards and had a drink after dinner. Not today. Today, he went to the basement, leaving me sitting at the table alone.

As I always did, I tried to pull my hand free of the handcuff. There was sure to be a time when he failed to tighten the restraints, and I was going to slip away from him. I never knew when that day would be, so I had to constantly try to free myself.

Several minutes passed before I began to feel funny. Light-headed, like my head was going to float off my body. My mouth became dry, and I felt nauseous. I broke out in a cold sweat. Feeling as though I were going to pass out, I put my left arm on the table and laid my head on it. I closed my eyes, hoping the feeling would pass.

I dreamed Ron picked me up and carried me away from the table. Cradled in his arms, I felt as though I were falling down into the cool darkness.

When I woke some time later, I was devastated to learn that it hadn't been a dream at all.

# 6

*So this was the basement*, I thought as I blinked to clear my vision. I'd spent all this time wondering what it was like and now I was here. And I wished like hell I wasn't.

The cold steel cuff was tight on my right wrist, the other end of the cuffs locked around a thick metal pipe that ran up the dirty concrete wall. I was lying on an old mattress on the floor. I had a pillow, though it smelled terrible. In fact, the whole basement smelled horrible. It was a sickening combination of dampness, rotten wood, dirt, stale water, and a medley of body odors.

I looked across the ceiling to the bare bulbs that hung from the beams. I counted four bulbs swinging from long cords, but only three of them were lit. One of them was considerably dimmer than the other two.

Raising my head from the pillow, I looked down my body and across the room. About ten feet past the end of the mattress I was lying on, was the stairs that led to the main floor. Where I should be. Where I would be, if I hadn't let my stupid mouth out-talk my ass.

The mattress that was my bed at the moment was nestled in the corner, a wall on two sides. The room opened up to my left, where I turned my attention.

That's when I saw Stephanie.

I quickly scooted myself into a sitting position, taking in the scene before me.

She was naked, just as she'd been the last time I'd seen her. I hadn't thought it was possible at the time, but she was dirtier now than then. Her arms were stretched out, each handcuffed to a chain. The chains were connected to some sort of metal hook that was anchored in the concrete floor. Her legs were outstretched in the same manner, spread wide apart.

"Stephanie," I said hoarsely. I cleared my throat and tried again. "Stephanie."

She didn't seem to hear me. If she was asleep, surely she would've been woken by the sound of my voice. I said her name again, louder this time, but she still didn't move. I was afraid he'd killed her. Focusing on her chest where her bare breasts were covered in dirt, bruises, and lacerations, I saw the rise and fall of her body, though it was quick and had no rhythm. She wasn't doing well.

She was far too thin. Her ribs were so visible, they appeared ready to poke through her skin at any second. Her hip bones protruded up at sharp angles. She looked to be nothing more than a skeleton with skin.

Figuring she needed whatever rest she could get, I put my back against the concrete wall, drew my knees up to my chest, and with one arm around my legs and the other handcuffed to a pipe, I waited. I hated to admit it to myself, but I suppose I was waiting on Ron. If he liked me as much as he said, he wouldn't leave me down here. Of course, if he liked me as much as he said, he probably wouldn't have put me down here in the first place, no matter how mouthy I had been.

What must've been a half hour went by before the door at the top of the wooden stairs opened and Ron appeared. When he saw that I was awake, he quickly closed the door behind him and nearly ran down the stairs.

At the bottom, he stopped and smiled at me. "Glad to have you back."

"Yeah. Good to be here. Listen, I was thinking maybe you could take me back upstairs with you."

"I'm afraid not. At least not for a while."

"Why not?"

"You need to be taught a lesson. I don't think you appreciate me or the things I've done for you. You don't realize how good you've had it, or how much worse you could have it. So I decided that the best way to teach you is to show you. And so you're here. Learning."

Okay. Surely, he wouldn't leave me down here long. A couple of days, maybe. I could pretend to have learned a lesson. I could act grateful. Speed things along a bit.

"I hate to see you down here, Nicole. I really do. But you must learn." He turned his attention to Stephanie. "She never learned. She never cared to learn. All she ever thought about was herself. She didn't care what I wanted or needed from her. And look at her now. In trying so desperately to save herself, she's only succeeding in killing herself."

"I think she needs to see a doctor."

"Oh I'm sure she does." He laughed. "But that's not going to happen. You know that, Nicole. Why do you insist on stating the obvious?"

Not wanting to do anything to cause my stay in the basement to be longer, I shut my mouth.

He walked over to Stephanie and stood between her open legs looking down on her.

"I'm sure she has broken bones," he said leaning down and squeezing a section of her right forearm, making the bones go in different directions.

I gasped and winced.

"I'm sure she has infected cuts," he said as he placed his hands, palms down, on either side of a terribly long and deep cut on her abdomen. I watched as he pulled open the wound, sickened by his actions. From the redness around the wound, I guessed that this wasn't the first time he'd spread apart her battered flesh. When he reached his hand down and gathered up some dirt from the concrete floor and dropped it into her gaping midsection, it left little wonder as to why it was infected. He wanted it to be. It was part of her lesson. Part of the torture he seemingly enjoyed inflicting on her.

Stephanie moaned, causing me to look back at her face, but she didn't wake.

Ron stood again. For a moment, he didn't speak or move. He just stood there between her outstretched legs. Then, he suddenly drew back his leg and kicked her in her crotch. With those heavy boot-like shoes of his, I had no doubts that it hurt terribly, but when Stephanie woke screaming, I knew for certain it had. After all, the ripping open of a flesh wound hadn't stirred her, but this had. With her legs spread open as they were and her feet and hands shackled, she had no way of defending herself. He stood there, kicking her crotch over and over, as hard as he could. He didn't even stop when the toe of his shoe became covered in her blood.

Was this the same man that made such great eggs? Was this the same man who could smile while losing at Gin Rummy? The same man who'd bought my tampons without a complaint? The man who'd laundered my clothes and folded them with such care? The very same man who folded the toilet paper to a point?

I watched as he kicked her, and I winced as she screamed, too shocked to look away.

Soon, her screams became so shrill they were like shards of glass scratching at my eardrums. Just when I thought I couldn't stand to hear her scream any more, he suddenly dropped to his knees and unfastened his slacks. He raped her while she screamed. Her screams seemed to excite him. The more she wailed, the harder at her he went. At the pinnacle of her screaming, the moments just before her voice cracked and went hoarse, he was thrusting at her so hard, it seemed as though he were trying to go through her and penetrate the floor. My girlie parts ached just watching. I couldn't even imagine the pain she was experiencing. I hoped like hell I'd never find out.

When he was finished, he was panting uncontrollably as sweat rolled down his face and fell from his chin. He slowly got back to his knees. As he put himself away and fastened his slacks, I saw the blood on his manhood. He stood and spit on her before walking back to the stairs. I thought he was leaving, but instead, he turned and sat on the bottom step, facing me from only a few feet away.

I trembled as I watched him run his hands through his hair and take deep breaths to calm his breathing. I shuddered when I noticed the torn pants and his bleeding knees inside. In his frenzy, he hadn't even felt his own wounds. Or maybe he had. Maybe he was one of those people that got off on pain.

He smiled at me. After what he'd just done to her, he was able to smile at me. Unbelievable.

"It wouldn't be that way with you, you know."

My mouth had gone dry. After swallowing a couple of times and working up some saliva, I was able to say, "Then why is it that way with her?"

"I've told you," he said, clearly irritated at having to repeat himself to me. "I never liked her. She isn't good company. All she cares about is herself. She's not like you."

I wanted to ask him what was so damn special about me, but I knew enough not to. All he ever said was I was good company, and I made good conversation. He liked me. He liked my personality, my attitude. I decided to leave it alone and just be happy that there was something about me he liked. Maybe his liking me would be my salvation. Surely, it would at the very least save me from the fate that had befallen Stephanie.

Ron left me naked in the basement. Normally, he allowed me to wear my panties. Not this time. He had taken everything. I still tried to look on the bright side. At least I wasn't tethered to the floor and spread apart the way Stephanie was. I could pull my knees up to my chest and cover myself somewhat. So at least there was that.

I tried to talk to Stephanie. After many times of saying her name, she finally turned her head slowly toward me. In her eyes, I saw nothing. Whether they were empty because she'd given up or because he'd stripped her of everything that made her a person, they were empty.

I asked her if she was okay, but she said nothing. A few minutes later, she closed her eyes.

The temperature in the basement was cool. With no clothes and no blanket, I did the best I could to stay warm. I curled up in the fetal position and eventually fell into a restless sleep.

Throughout my life, I'd occasionally had nightmares. Usually, I was being chased by a man trying to kill me. Sometimes, he stabbed or shot me, and I always woke right before I died. This time, when I woke, the nightmare that haunted my sleep was nothing compared to the nightmare taking place only a few feet from me.

I slowly rolled over, every muscle in my body aching. Blinking rapidly to clear my vision, I focused on Stephanie and what was happening to her. I wished I'd stayed asleep.

Ron was beating her with a fireplace poker. Over and over, he raised the poker and brought it down with a thud against Stephanie's frail body. But that wasn't the scary part. The scary part of the scene was the lack of movement coming from Stephanie.

I watched carefully but saw no signs of life. She didn't flinch. She didn't yell or scream. She did nothing. She was dead. She had to be.

After many more blows to her lifeless body, Ron stopped. He threw his head up toward the ceiling. I could see his back and shoulders heaving as he gasped for air. With his back to me, I couldn't see his face, but I didn't think I wanted to.

Moments later, I didn't have a choice. He whirled around and glared at me. He raced across the room toward me and in a flash he was standing beside my mattress looking down at me, still holding the poker.

"This is your fault," he screamed, pointing the poker at my face.

Still pushing away sleep, I asked, "How the hell is this my fault?"

"I went to your room this morning to get you up and dressed. But you weren't there," he said, his voice rising and falling as he spoke.

"No. I'm not there. Because you brought me down to this dungeon," I screamed up at him. "I didn't ask you to bring me down here. I didn't want this. So it's your fault," I yelled, clearly having learned nothing yet.

His nostrils flared with anger. My attention focused on the poker and I thought maybe I should stop yelling at him. I knew I should, but I also knew that my back-talking sassiness was what he liked most about me. It was a fine line that was sure to be the downfall of me once I stepped across it at the wrong time.

For a while longer, he stood over me, though he had at least lowered the poker and now held it at his side. I watched as he slowly calmed down. His nostrils stopped flaring, his chest quit heaving with his heavy breathing, and he finally relaxed his grip on the poker.

As he calmed down, so did I, though I was still terrified. I'd watched him kill Stephanie. And if she was already dead before I woke up, then I'd watched him beat the hell out of a corpse. Either way, I knew I wasn't dealing with the average feller. This man was truly a psychopath, flying from one extreme to the next in the blink of an eye. Professionals who had spent years studying and researching people like him didn't know how to deal with them, so how was I supposed to know how to handle him? And unlike the pros, my life depended on it.

He tossed the poker aside, but too far for me to reach. Even if I turned myself around and stretched my body as far as it would stretch, I wouldn't have been able to reach it with my foot. Even in his madness, he was smart enough to know not to leave it where I could get to it. That made him even more dangerous in my opinion because even when it seemed that he'd lost all touch with reality and his thoughts and emotions, he still knew what not to do. Scary.

Thinking of a way to get back on his good side and back to the main floor of the house, I asked, "What are you going to do now?" I hoped he didn't detect the tremor in my voice.

"I'm going to have to get rid of it. It's going to start smelling soon, and I don't want you to have to smell that."

Good. He was looking out for me, in a sick sort of way. All hope wasn't lost. I felt certain that soon, maybe later today or tomorrow, he'd take me back upstairs. He still liked me enough to not want me trapped down here with the smell of a rotting corpse. Of course, my hope was destroyed when I asked for food.

"Ron, what time is it?"

"Why? Do you have somewhere you need to be?"

"Yeah. I need to be at home with my family, but since that isn't possible, I was just wondering."

Glancing at his watch, he answered, "Seven thirty."

"I'm hungry, and I need to pee."

After staring at me for a few seconds, he put his foot against a plastic bowl that set on the floor between Stephanie's body and me and pushed it my way. I watched the bowl slide toward me and stop a foot or so away from the mattress. I reached out and pulled it the rest of the way to me. Looking inside, I thought he was joking. He must be.

"What's this?" I asked, looking up at him.

50

"If you're hungry, eat that. It's what I fed Stephanie until she quit eating. Poor thing starved herself to death," he said looking over his shoulder at her body.

"No, I'm pretty sure you beat her to death with that there poker." When I saw him snap his head back to face me, I quickly moved on. "If this is what she had to eat, no wonder she wouldn't eat it. What is it anyway?"

"It's dog food."

"Are you serious?" I looked into the bowl again. It didn't look like dog food. Of course, with the maggots and flies covering it, who could tell what it was?

"It's the good kind. None of that cheap stuff. Besides, dog food is required by the FDA to be fit for human consumption. People eat it during recessions like this. It's fine."

"It's got bugs all over it."

"Yes. It's been down here a while. Let's see, she quit eating over a week ago, maybe close to two weeks. Pick them off. Or eat them. They're full of protein."

"You know what else is full of protein? Steak and eggs. Why don't you run upstairs and make that happen for me?"

He laughed. "There's the girl I love."

Love? What happened to like? I didn't dwell on the use of terms. What captured my attention was that I was back in his good graces. One step closer to getting back upstairs.

He headed up the stairs.

"Are you going to make me something to eat?"

"Eat what's in the bowl, Nicole. When you're down here, you don't get the luxury of my cooking. And if you need to pee, do it on the floor." With that, he went through the doorway and closed the door behind him, leaving me alone in the basement with a full bladder, a battered corpse, and a bowl of rotten dog food.

# 7

I waited and waited for Ron to return, but he didn't. My belly growled, but I ignored it. If Stephanie could go nearly two weeks without food, surely I could go a couple of days. That should be long enough for him to allow me back upstairs.

Funny how I had begged him to let me go home, and now I was begging him to let me go upstairs. The worse my situation got, the better off I realized I'd had it before.

Eventually, I could hold my pee no longer. I looked for a bucket or a hole or anything, but other than the bowl containing the dog food, there was nothing. So I squatted on the mattress with my butt hung over the edge and let it go. I cried as I peed, having been reduced to such animalistic ways, but there was no other way. Beside the mattress was better than on it.

After I'd drained my bladder, I sat on the mattress and looked at the mess I'd made as it slowly crept across the concrete floor. As it made its way to the drain in the center of the room, it pooled around Stephanie's heel. I felt horrible that she had to lie in my piss. Damn Ron.

At some point, I fell asleep. I had no way of keeping track of time in the basement. If there were any windows, they were tightly covered and let in no light. I never knew what day it was or what time it was.

I woke to the feel of someone's hand on my butt. Once again, I was curled in the fetal position to stay as warm as I could. I opened my eyes but didn't move. Focusing on the feel of the touch, I ruled out the possibility of a bug or a rodent. It was definitely a human. A disturbing image flashed through my mind of Stephanie's cold corpse crawling across the floor and touching me. I quickly rolled onto my back to find that Ron was on his knees beside me.

"Will you have me now?" he asked.

Immediately, I answered no.

In a huff, he got up. In the dim light of the bare bulbs, I saw that he was naked. And excited. And now, angry.

He paced back and forth for a little bit, mumbling under his breath something I couldn't make out. I watched him closely, afraid this would be the time he raped me. And if it was, I'd still consider myself lucky that I wasn't Stephanie.

I watched in amazement that even in his anger and frustration, he kept his erection. It bobbed around in front of him as he angrily stomped back and forth across the room. Had this been a movie I was watching from the comfort of my own home, I would've surely laughed. But here, in this moment, it was the farthest thing from funny.

Then, he saw Stephanie. With no more than a second's worth of consideration, he walked over to her and got on his knees. With her arms and legs still shackled to the floor, spread wide, he had his way with her.

As if it wasn't disturbing enough to watch him rape a dead woman, I listened as he said my name over and over while doing it. With each thrust of his hips, he said, "Nicole. Nicole. Nicole." As he climaxed, he said my name again. This time, it was loud. A long, terrifying howl of my name, sure to haunt me in my sleep.

And that wasn't even the creepy part.

Worse than watching him rape a dead woman, worse than him repeatedly saying my name while raping a dead woman, was the fact that he stared at me the whole time. His eyes never left mine while he defiled the woman he'd murdered so violently.

53

My skin broke out in gooseflesh, my throat tightened, my stomach knotted, and my heart pounded.

He got up from her and walked past me without saying anything. I watched him walk slowly up the stairs. When he closed the door behind him, I released the breath I'd been holding. I noticed I was crying, so I gave in and let it go, crying harder than I'd ever cried before.

The severity of the situation was starting to sink in on me. All thoughts of controlling the situation were gone now. All hopes of being let go were gone along with them. I wasn't capable of handling someone like him. I had no training in dealing with people with mental problems. I don't know if anyone had the training it would take to deal with Ron. He scared me more than anything I'd ever encountered, either in real life or in my nightmares.

As I fell asleep, I was grateful for the sweet release sleep brought to me. Even if my dreams were nightmares, it'd be less frightening than my reality.

I woke some time later to the sounds of Ron beating Stephanie's lifeless body, but when I rolled over, I was alone in the basement. Well, alone with Stephanie's body. Ron wasn't in the room. I must've been having a nightmare. The sad part was the nightmare had been a reality just hours before.

When I escaped, I was going to have to get two jobs to pay for the therapy I was going to need to deal with this trauma.

The next time I woke, it was to the loud clanging sound of what reminded me of metal striking metal. I quickly sat up and scooted backward until I felt the cold wall at my back. From there, I watched Ron work.

He had an axe high above his head. I watched as he brought it down hard, slicing through Stephanie's outstretched arm near where it connected to her shoulder. I gasped, but if he heard me, he ignored me and kept on chopping. First one arm, and then the other. Then, he moved to her legs, chopping each of them off close to the hip.

With each strike of the axe came the sound of a snapping bone, followed by the clink of the metal striking the concrete floor. Also with each strike of the axe, I jumped and closed my eyes.

After decapitating the torso, he tossed the axe to the floor and wiped his forehead with the back of his hand.

He glanced over at me and saw that I was watching him. "Dirty work," he said.

I could only nod stiffly.

After unlocking the restraints of her wrists and ankles, he placed each of her limbs in a separate black trash bag and tied it tightly. He did the same for her head and torso, though the torso wasn't as easy for him as the smaller pieces had been.

Two by two, he carried the bags up the steps while I watched in silence.

When all the bags were gone from the basement, he returned. Exhausted, he sat on the bottom step, facing me.

"Are you afraid, Nicole?"

I wasn't sure what to say. Did he want me to be afraid? The wrong answer may be my ticket to a trash bag, so I weighed my words carefully.

"I'm afraid that you'll end up not liking me enough to put me in a trash bag like you did her."

"Nonsense. I told you, I didn't like her from the beginning. She wasn't you. And you aren't her. As long as you don't make the same mistakes as she did, you'll be fine."

"I'm thirsty. And hungry."

He pointed to the bowl of rotten dog food. "You have food right there. As for water, I'll get you a drink in a moment. I must rest now. I'm afraid I'm not as young as I used to be." He laughed. "That's a silly expression, don't you think? After all, none of us are ever as young as we used to be. In fact, I'm not as young as I was when I said that." He laughed again, more to himself than anything. Then, he said, "Tell me, Nicole. Did watching me with her stir up any feelings of jealousy?"

I stared at him, confused as to what he meant.

Seeing my confusion, he elaborated. "I mean, were you jealous that I was being with her in that way? Did you wish it were you underneath me?"

I felt there was no right answer here. To say yes might make him rape me. To say no might make him angry enough to use the poker on me. It was a no-win situation. No matter what I said, I was certain it would be wrong. But I had to say something, so I went with, "No."

He shook his head. "That's a shame. But you know I wanted it to be you. I came to you, needing to be with you in that way. And you denied me. What was I to do, Nicole? I am only a man with manly desires. I have wants and needs. These are things you must understand. You have a husband, after all. Surely, you know how it works."

"It's different with my husband."

"Different? How?"

"With him, I want him just as much as he wants me."

He thought for a moment and then asked, "Are you saying that you don't want me?"

Another trap. Unsure of what to say, I said nothing.

"Nicole?" he shouted. "Are you saying that you don't want me?"

His voice echoed off the walls of the basement. His eyes were getting that wild look to them again.

Not wanting to enrage him but not wanting to encourage him either, I said, "No. At least not yet."

He calmed a little and asked, "What do you mean by not yet?"

"Well, I haven't known you that long. What kind of girl do you think I am? I can't just go around giving myself to every man who wants me, now can I? That would make me no better than Stephanie."

Completely relaxed and back to the happy Ron that made a mean sandwich, he smiled and nodded. "That's my girl. In time, I'm sure you'll grow to want me as much as I want you. Then, it will be sweet." He nodded at the spot where Stephanie's body had been. "Until then, I'll need someone to fill in."

I watched as Ron walked across the basement to a utility sink. Hanging on the wall beside it was a yellow garden hose. He took it from its place, connected it to the faucet, and turned on the water. He walked across the room to me, stopping a few feet away from my mattress. I waited for him to come closer, but he didn't.

"You thirsty?" he asked.

I nodded.

He unscrewed the nozzle from the end of the hose. The water came out and fell to the floor in splatters.

"Come and get it."

Handcuffed to the pipe, I couldn't get far. I got up on my knees and leaned as far as I could toward him. It wasn't far enough. I leaned farther, causing great pain to my right arm and wrist, which was twisted around behind me in an awkward position. Had I not been so damn thirsty, I would've told him to shove that hose up his ass.

He pulled up on the hose quickly, creating an arc of water that hit my face. It was cold. Shockingly cold. I gasped, and then licked my lips, getting all the water I could.

He laughed. I didn't.

Again, he jerked up on the hose and splashed my face. Again, I licked the water from my lips.

"Nicole, if you want me to contain my passion for you, you really must stop acting so provocatively. You're exciting me."

"Well maybe if you'd just give me a drink of water, this wouldn't be a problem. And if you didn't have me down here naked, maybe you could contain yourself more."

Smiling, he stepped forward and let me drink from the hose. I drank and drank until I thought I would throw up. I wanted to drink more then, but he walked away, taking the precious water with him.

He twisted the nozzle back on the hose. Water came out, this time with pressure pushing it. As he began spraying the floor, washing away Stephanie's blood, I scooted back against the wall. Drawing my legs up to cover my chest, I watched him work.

"One of the reasons I bought this house was the drain in the basement floor. Very convenient, wouldn't you say?"

I didn't answer.

"I'm sure it's there in case the washing machine overflows or leaks, but it is so handy for washing away blood. This house has paid for itself many times over with this drain. Money well spent."

I watched the dirt and blood slide across the floor and disappear down the drain. I wondered if one day, a woman would sit hand-cuffed to this very pipe and watch in fear as my blood swirled away down the drain.

I felt drops of liquid fall from my face and hit my arm, and I wondered if it was tears or the water he'd sprayed on me.

When he was finished cleaning the floor, he brought the hose back to me. I quickly got up on my knees again, begging for water. This time, when he unscrewed the nozzle, he let the water pour down on me, running down my chin, my breasts, my belly, and dripping onto the floor and the mattress.

He squatted down in front of me and watched the water run over my chest. I didn't care. I was drinking as much as I could while what I couldn't drink ran down my body. If he wanted to watch, that was his problem.

Even when he reached out and cupped my breast, I ignored him and continued to drink the disgusting, rubbery tasting water.

Finally, he stood up. "If I don't find someone to fill in for you quickly, you're going to have to learn to want me." He reached into his pants and adjusted himself before turning and walking away, taking the hose back to its spot on the wall.

As he was leaving the basement, he stopped at the foot of the mattress. "I'm going to dispose of this trash. I'll be back. It may be a while, though. Try to miss me while I'm away."

"Wait," I said quickly as he ascended the stairs. "Can I get a blanket? And some food? And water? And a bucket to use as a toilet?"

Halfway up the steps, he turned to me. "That's a lot of requests coming from a girl in the basement. You can pee on the floor. I'll wash it when I get back. You've got food, Nicole. Eat that. As for the blanket, you should have enough nice thoughts of me to keep you warm. And as for water, there's a thunderstorm due tonight or tomorrow. When it rains, water seeps into the basement. That should hold you until I return. I'll see you soon." And with that, he disappeared into the main floor, closing the door behind him.

Just how long did he plan to be gone? At least a couple days from the way he talked.

I wanted to cry. But I wouldn't let myself until I'd thought through the situation I was in now. If this bowl of rotten dog food was all I had to eat, it was going to have to do.

Pulling the bowl to me, I felt my stomach rumble. I wasn't going to eat it yet. I was just preparing for when the time came that I had to.

As disgusting as it was, I reached in and began pulling out the maggots. One by one, I pulled them from the bowl, placed them on the floor, and stomped them with the heel of my foot. When the bowl was free of the white, wriggling worms, I slid it aside. I sat back and looked around the dank room.

I felt myself falling apart and did nothing to stop it. Knowing I should conserve my energy and fluids, I cried.

# 8

I had no way of knowing how long it was before Ron returned. It could've been several hours. It could've been a couple of days. The minutes all ran together in the basement with no way of telling time.

All I knew for sure was that the things I'd had to do to survive were things I wasn't proud of doing.

I didn't want to lick the water off the concrete walls as the rain seeped in. But I did. Until my tongue was raw from scraping it against the rough concrete.

I didn't want to shit on the floor beside my bed. But I did. Three times.

I didn't want to eat that dog food. And I didn't. That was still a line I wasn't able to cross. Though my stomach rumbled and I was weak, I held out. Ignoring the voice in my head that shouted out for me to just close my eyes and eat it, I waited. I still had hope that he would bring me food.

Turns out, Ron did bring me something, but it wasn't the food I was craving.

I woke to Ron shaking me. When I opened my eyes, he smiled down at me. It took everything I had, but I pushed myself up and sat with my back to the wall.

"Did you miss me?" he asked, smiling.

Hungry and hopeful, I nodded.

"Good. I knew you would. I see you haven't eaten. Is there a reason?"

"Yeah. It's rotten dog food."

"So you'd rather starve than eat old dog food? Interesting. Are you often stubborn, or is it just when it comes to what you eat?"

"I'm not picky. I just won't eat rotten food. Would you please bring me a sandwich or something?"

He considered this for a moment and said, "No. Girls in the basement eat basement food. If you want a sandwich, then you must learn your lesson."

"I have," I said quickly.

"Oh have you?" he asked suspiciously. "What lesson have you learned?"

Shit.

"Well, I've learned that I shouldn't make you angry."

He nodded.

"And I shouldn't talk back to you."

He shook his head. "I'm afraid you're wrong. It seems you haven't learned your lesson yet. But don't worry." He kissed the top of my head and stood. "You will. Until then, I'm afraid this is your dinner," he said, nudging the bowl with his foot. "It won't be so bad. Remember, it could always be worse."

That was no lie.

It wasn't until Ron was gone that I noticed the woman. Had she not moaned, I may not have noticed her.

She was chained where Stephanie had been. She was taller than Stephanie and had more meat on her bones. Her hair was light brown and curly. She was also naked, just as Stephanie had been, and just as I was now.

"Hey," I said. "Hey, are you awake? Can you hear me?"

Her eyes fluttered and she looked at me. She struggled against her restraints, but she could've struggled till the end of time and it wouldn't have done any good.

"Where am I?" she asked. She had a raspy voice, the kind women have when they've spent their lives smoking. She looked to be in her fifties, so she must've gotten an early start.

"You're in the basement of a psychopathic asshole."

"How'd I get here?"

"I don't know."

"I was in a bar. Dancing on a table. Some guy helped me down. He held out his hand. I thought that was so sweet. I sat with him and had some drinks. He flirted with me. I decided to go home with him. I don't even remember leaving the bar."

"What's your name?"

"Melinda."

"I'm Nicole. Are you married?"

"Yes. When he finds out this john kidnapped me, he'll kill him," she said angrily.

"John? You're a prostitute?"

"Yeah."

"And your husband knows?"

"It was his idea. We needed money and that's a sure, quick way to get some."

"It's also a sure, quick way to end up restrained in a basement."

"Honey, I wish you'd have told me that yesterday." She pulled against the chains again, but still no results. "How long have you been here?"

"I'm not sure. More than a month, I know."

"Shit. I better not be here that long."

"There was a woman before you. She'd been here a long time."

"Where's she now?"

How could I tell her? To tell her what had happened to Stephanie would be to tell her what was going to happen to her.

"She didn't make it," I said simply.

"The son of a bitch killed her, didn't he?" she asked.

It surprised me that she would ask such a question so bluntly. But judging by the way she looked and talked, and by her line of work, I was sure she'd seen a lot of stuff. There was no sense in sugar-coating the situation.

"Yes. And he wasn't nice about it."

"Of course he wasn't. Assholes like him are never nice about nothing. I had a feeling he was gonna want some of that kinky stuff.

For the right price, I'm up for anything, though. Anything except this." A few minutes later, she asked, "When he does you, how bad is it?"

"What do you mean?"

"I mean, how rough is he? Does he like it in the backdoor? How big is he?"

Wow. She didn't mess around. "I don't know."

"What do you mean you don't know? You've been here over a month and he hasn't done you yet?"

"He's tried."

"How'd you stop him? How could a little thing like you fight him off?"

Fortunately, the door opened at the top of the steps and Ron appeared. I was glad. I had no idea how to tell her the reason he hadn't had sex with me yet. I wasn't even sure of the reason myself.

Ron came down the stairs smiling. Stepping off the bottom step, he looked at us and asked, "How's my girls?"

Neither of us spoke.

"Come on, ladies. Don't be so glum. It can't be all that bad, can it?"

"Let me go, you prick, and I'll tell my husband not to kill you."

"Do you think your husband plans to kill me?" he asked, walking toward her. "Or do you think he's happy that I've taken such a foul-mouthed burden off his shoulders? After all, you're just a whore. No one cares what happens to you."

"My husband does," she yelled.

"Does he? Then why does he sit idly by while you let any man that comes along have his way with you? In fact, why does he offer you to these men, recruiting them, so to speak?"

She said nothing.

"I'll tell you why," Ron said calmly. He knelt down beside her head and leaned over her. "Because he doesn't care about you," he yelled. "He cares less about you than any other whore on the street. You're a worthless bag of spent sperm and deserve nothing more than for me to kill you right now."

He slapped her across the face. The loud, sudden smack made me jump.

She didn't cry, though. In her line of work, she'd probably had more than her fair share of getting slapped around by some dickhead.

He smiled. Then, he stood and came over to me. Kneeling beside my mattress, he stroked my hair.

"And you. How are you?"

"I'm okay," I whispered.

"Are you?" he asked as he kissed my forehead. "You're just as beautiful as you were when I left you. Although you seem to have lost a bit of weight. I don't like that, Nicole. I don't want to see you looking like Stephanie. That's very unattractive on a woman, don't you think?"

I nodded.

"You need to eat, don't you agree?"

I nodded.

"I'll tell you what. You eat what's in that bowl, and I'll make you something nice for dinner. Okay?"

Again, I nodded. What else could I do?

He kissed my forehead. "That's my girl. I'll come down later and check on you." He glanced back over his shoulder, then whispered, "Don't let that one rub off on you. She's a hard pill to swallow."

He stood and walked out of the basement, leaving me to eat the contents of the bowl.

# 9

I sat with my back against the wall. In my lap was the bowl of rotten dog food. Even from this distance, the smell was horrible. I stared at it, listening to my stomach rumble, and tried to talk myself into eating it. I reminded myself that if I ate it, I would have a nice meal for dinner.

Using my left hand, I picked up a piece and brought it to my lips. I opened my mouth and slowly put the piece in, holding it above my tongue. Just before I dropped it onto my tongue, I had a better idea.

Lifting up the edge of the mattress on my right side, the side against the wall, I dumped the dog food on the floor and covered it with the mattress. Now Ron would think I ate it and make some real food. I didn't like to think of myself as a genius, but it was starting to look I just might be.

I set the bowl back on the floor and waited for his return. But then I got to thinking. Ron was a tricky devil. He surely wouldn't be fooled so easily. What if he didn't believe me? What if he looked around to see if I'd dumped it? Worse still, what if he smelled my breath and didn't detect the stench of the dog food?

Working myself into a near panic, I reached under the mattress and pulled out a piece. I quickly ate it. Holding my breath, I chomped it a couple of times and quickly swallowed it. I waited a while before I breathed through my nose to avoid tasting it.

I did all this with my back to Melinda. I didn't trust her. What if she told on me to win Ron's favor and try to save herself? I wouldn't throw her under the bus like that, but she seemed just the type to do it to me.

Eventually, Ron came back. I waited as patiently as I could while he cleaned up my pile of excrement. When he'd picked it up and sprayed the floor with cleaner, he finally asked me about it.

"I see we ate our food."

Behind him, Melinda struggled against her restraints and cursed aloud.

"Yeah. It was disgusting. But at least I had something to eat." It was weak and I was sure he'd see through it, but I wanted more than just something good to eat. I wanted out of this basement. And if I had to make him think I'd learned a lesson, then so be it.

He smiled at me. "I knew you'd learn, Nicole. I had a feeling about you as soon as I put my arm around you in the parking lot of the mall. I could just tell you were special."

As he scrubbed the floor beside the mattress, I considered kicking him in the face. I didn't of course. That would've been stupid. I'd never get out of the basement doing things like that. Instead, I sat there silently and watched him until he was finished.

"Do you feel that you've learned something down here?"

"Yes, I do."

"And what have you learned?"

"I've learned to appreciate not only you, but the things you do for me. I've also learned that it's never as bad as it could be." I threw that last part in for good measure. After all, those were his words. That should show him that I listen to him and agree with him.

He nodded and smiled. Then, he leaned toward me.

"Are you ready to have me yet?"

"Not exactly," I said slowly. When I saw the look on his face, I quickly added, "I still haven't got to know you that well. I mean,

I've been down here and you've been so busy, we haven't spent a lot of time together."

I watched as the smile that had nearly faded when I started talking reappeared.

"You're right." He opened his mouth to say more, but Melinda began to scream at him.

He quickly stood and walked across the room. From a cabinet hanging over the utility sink, he produced a skinny pole-type object with two prongs sticking out the end. I wasn't sure exactly what it was. I wasn't sure until I saw him use it.

With this object in his hand, he walked to Melinda and stood over her. "Do you like screaming?" he asked.

"Yes," she screamed up at him.

He leaned down and touched the prong end to her bare belly. Oh, how she screamed then. In fact, each time he touched it to her skin, she screamed and thrashed and howled in pain. That's when I figured out the device was an electric cattle prod. I'd seen them used before, but never on a human.

"Do you like screaming now?" he asked, as his eyes took on a crazed look.

Through her screams and clenched teeth, I heard her try to say no to him. Either he didn't hear her or he chose to ignore her, and he stuck the prongs to her skin a few more times.

Finally, he stopped sending the volts through her body and left her writhing on the floor. He returned the cattle prod to the cabinet and came to me. Squatted beside me, the crazy look that I'd seen in his eyes as he shocked her was gone, replaced by the affectionate look he always gave me. The one that made my skin crawl.

"Do you feel that you should be allowed back upstairs?"

I nodded.

"Can I trust you to have dinner with me at the table and act civilized?"

Pushing my luck, I asked, "Haven't I always been civilized?"

"Indeed you have, Nicole. Most civilized."

Then, he leaned in and kissed me on the mouth. It shocked me because he'd never kissed my mouth before, but it absolutely startled me when I felt his tongue slide in between my lips and swirl around in my mouth. The urge to bite him was powerful, but I managed to fight it. A few seconds later, he withdrew his tongue and leaned back. I watched as he licked his lips, clearly tasting me. He smiled and nodded, and I was certain then that he'd been checking for traces of dog food.

From his front pocket, he pulled the key to the handcuffs that bound me to the water pipe. He leaned across me and unlocked the one secured around the pipe. He helped me to my feet and led me up the stairs, one hand on my wrist, the other around my waist.

I couldn't help but be excited. I was still trapped here in this house with a madman, but at least I was out of the basement. I'd successfully made him think I'd learned whatever lesson he thought he was teaching me. When I got home, I'd have to a clear a shelf for my Academy Award. Until then, I'd have to continue to make him think I'd learned something in the basement.

In reality, I had learned many things down there. I'd learned that he was far more dangerous than I'd previously thought. I'd learned that a few whacks of an axe would completely dismember a body. I also learned that when repeatedly shocked with an electric cattle prod, human flesh smells like burning bacon. I learned licking seeping rain water from a concrete wall chafed the tongue. I learned that necrophilia existed, though I'd previously failed to believe anyone would ever stoop to such grotesque levels. Most importantly, I'd learned that Ron was a sick, twisted psychopath who flew from one extreme to another, and who enjoyed inflicting torture on other people. He saw joy where others found pain.

Yes, I had learned many things down there.

# 10

Once we were in the hallway upstairs, Ron turned to me and said, "You smell most foul."

Trying to keep up the attitude he liked, I said, "Don't hold back, Ron. Tell me how you really feel."

He led me to the bathroom, opened the door, and turned on the light. As he removed the cuff from my wrist, he said, "You take a shower and I'll bring your things. Once you've cleaned up, I'll make us that dinner I promised you." He smiled.

I went in the bathroom and happily, though weakly, showered. When I was finished, I pulled back the shower curtain and saw my things stacked neatly on the counter. Feeling better than I had in quite some time, I rushed to them.

The first thing I did was put on my clothes. I'd been naked for too long. Then, I brushed my teeth longer than I ever had in my life. While I scrubbed away the gross taste and germs, I wondered how effective a toothbrush would be as a weapon. Then, I combed my hair.

When I opened the door, Ron was standing there waiting for me. He filled the doorway, as if he thought I might've had the strength to attempt to flee. I'd barely had the strength to clean myself. Fleeing was out of the question. At least for now.

After he snapped the cuff back on my right wrist, he led me to the kitchen where he once again snapped the other cuff to the underside of the table. He then set about making our dinner.

While he worked, I rested my head on my arm on the table. I must've dozed off because the next thing I know, he was shaking me gently and holding a plate of hot food.

My eyes snapped open at the delicious aroma. I sat up quickly, allowing Ron to set the plate where my head had been.

Ron had kept his word and made me something nice for dinner. Steak, mashed potatoes with gravy, and green beans. For dessert, chocolate mousse. I shoveled food into my mouth with the spoon until I was certain I would burst open, spilling the contents onto the floor.

After he'd cleared the table and started the dishes in the dishwasher, he asked, "Would you care to partake of a game of cards?"

"I would, but I'm exhausted. Would you mind if I just went to bed?" It was true. I was so tired I could hardly keep my eyes open.

He smiled and nodded. "Sure. There's always tomorrow, isn't there?"

As he led me to bed, undressed me, and restrained my arms, I kept hearing his words echoing through my mind.

There's always tomorrow, there's always tomorrow...

Was that my life now? Stuck here in this house with him while he killed women in the basement? Thinking of ways to keep him liking me, and yet keep him from having me. Always trying to think faster than him, trying to guess his next move. Trying to do or say whatever would set him off the least. Jumping in my skin every time he moved, wondering if this was the time he'd turn his anger on me.

I couldn't do it. I couldn't live like that forever. I had to get out of this house and away from him. I didn't know how or when, but I knew that I had to. But any attempts I was to make would have to wait until I'd regained my strength.

I was pretty certain that while I was naked and strapped to the bed, I felt his hands not only fondling my breasts, but sliding up and down my thighs. I fell asleep quickly, but I never felt him touching my crotch while I was awake. As crazy as he was, there was no telling what he did after I drifted off.

The next morning, I woke to find Ron standing beside the bed. His arms were folded across his chest. Though he was looking at me, he didn't seem to see me. He was too lost in thought. In fact, he didn't even notice that I was awake for a few minutes, which was more than enough time for me to notice the blood under his fingernails.

At first, I thought I was imagining it. After all, he was meticulous about cleaning. Surely, he wouldn't walk around with fresh blood caked under his nails. But after blinking to clear my vision, I clearly identified it as blood. Fresh blood. Some of it still seemed wet.

I wouldn't have brought myself to his attention at all. I would've continued lying there while he remained lost in thought. But I really had to pee.

"Ron."

Nothing.

"Ron."

When he spoke, it was quiet. Too quiet for me to clearly hear. But after concentrating hard on what I had managed to hear, I deduced that he'd said, "I'll just kill her."

I wasn't sure what to make of that. Was he referring to me or Melinda? Or maybe he was remembering Stephanie. I had no idea what to think.

On the verge of pissing the bed, I said, "Ron," with more force than before.

This did the trick. His eyes cleared and he focused on me.

"Good morning."

"I really have to pee," I said squirming a little.

"I'm sure you do," he said without moving.

Several seconds passed and he still hadn't moved. He just kept standing there smiling at me.

"Ron, I really have to go."

"I know."

"Do you think you could undo these cuffs and let me use the bathroom?"

"Sure." He kept smiling, and he kept not moving.

71

"Ron, you're really starting to piss me off here. I have got to go."

"I know you do, Nicole." His smile, which had been up to this point a regular smile, was now the smile I would expect a psychopath to have. There was nothing in those crazy eyes of his. His smile had an evil undertone.

Angry, I said, "Do you want me to piss the bed?"

"Do you think that's wise?"

"Do you think it's wise to leave me laying here, knowing I have to pee?"

"Do what you feel you must. I believe you don't need to go as badly as you think you do. It's all a matter of the mind, Nicole."

"No. It's a matter of the bladder. The damn thing's full and screaming for me to let it out. But I can't do that if the asshole with the key won't unlock the handcuffs."

"Really, Nicole, that language isn't becoming of a woman of mine."

"A woman of yours?" I asked in a snotty tone. I faintly remembered that I was supposed to be on his side, buying myself time to find a way out. It was hard to do at the moment, though.

"Yes. You're a woman of mine. And you really shouldn't say things that a woman of Melinda's sort would say."

"Well if I'm a woman of yours, you really shouldn't leave me here in pain, begging you to use the toilet," I said as I squeezed my legs together as best I could.

"Maybe you're right. But maybe you need to learn control. You need to learn to control your body, Nicole. It's mind over matter."

"Now it's piss over foam, you dickhead. I just pissed the bed because of you." I couldn't help but cry. I was ashamed of myself. I hated him. How could he do that to me? How could I let him?

Quickly, he jerked the blanket off my naked body and watched as the sheet grew darker in a growing pool around me. He watched until I was finished. All I could do was cry. I couldn't hide my face. The best I could do was turn my head to the right as far as I could.

As my thighs and butt grew warmer, I hated him more and more. I hadn't wet the bed since I was three, yet here I was at twenty-eight, wetting the hell out of a bed because of him. If I ever managed to pull my hand free of the cuff, I'd kill him, even if I had to do it with my bare hands.

"Do you need to release your bowels, as well?" he asked.

"No. There's enough shit going on in this room," I snapped.

He chuckled. One of these days, I'd knock the chuckle right out of him.

He finally released me from the bed and led me to the bathroom for my usual morning routine. I took longer today than usual. I stayed in the shower until the hot water ran cold. I brushed my teeth until my gums bled. I combed my hair until my scalp burned. Fuck him. He made me piss the bed. The least I could do to him was make him stand in the hall and wait for me.

# 11

Two days after I'd pissed the bed, Ron sat across the table from me. We'd finished a delicious breakfast of fried eggs and bacon and were halfway through a game of Gin Rummy. I was winning.

"I have a surprise for you, Nicole." I could tell by the way his face lit up he was excited.

"Really?" I asked as unenthusiastically as possible.

"Yes," he said getting up from the table. "I'll be right back." He briskly walked out of the kitchen.

As I listened to his footsteps fade down the hallway, I tried to pull my hand free of the handcuff. I struggled with it until I heard his footsteps return.

He held something behind his back and sat in his chair. Smiling, he revealed that he was holding a stack of papers.

"What is it?"

"What is it?" he asked as if I'd just asked the world's silliest question. "You know what it is."

"You're right," I said. "Of course I know what it is. I just have a horrible habit of asking questions I already know the answer to. It's kind of a hobby of mine."

He shook his head and smiled. "I sure love having you here."

"I'm so lucky."

"It's the book."

This piqued my interest. "The book? The book I'm supposed to be helping you with?"

"Yes, and you are helping me, Nicole. I've learned so much from you. You really have made this character come to life for me. She's more than just a name on a page to me now. When I think of her, I think of you. I suppose that's how it will always be," he said fondly.

I said nothing.

"Would you like to read it?"

I considered reading it. I wasn't sure if I should or not. It would probably be a good insight into the mind of a maniac, but did I want to see that? Wasn't it bad enough knowing what I knew about him already? Did I really want a behind-the-scenes look at the workings of a monster?

"Yes," I said.

"Well you can't," he snapped.

"Why not?"

"I don't want you to read it until it's finished. I'd like it to be a surprise to you."

"Why the hell would you ask me to read it if you weren't going to let me?" I asked angrily.

"I just wanted to know that you wanted to read it. And now I know," he said smiling. He put the stack of papers on the floor by his feet, out of my sight and reach, but not out of my mind.

I couldn't help myself. "I hope you get a paper cut from those papers and it gets infected."

He laughed. "I'm sure you do, Nicole."

A while later, I asked, "Do you have a television?"

"No. They're nonsensical and impractical. They waste a lot of valuable time."

"They don't waste time. People waste time watching the stupid crap they put on TV. But there's a lot of good stuff on there too. Lots of educational programs. For example, and this should interest you, there are several shows devoted to serial killers."

"Is that so?" he asked, obviously amused with me. I'd thought I was treading on some thin ice making such a statement in such a crass way, but it seemed to only entertain him.

"Yeah. And not just serial killers. Psychopaths, schizophrenics, delusional people, pretty much all kinds of whack jobs."

He chuckled. "Maybe I should invest in a television after all."

"You should."

He looked at me with enough affection to turn my stomach, and then asked, "Did you watch a lot of television?"

I winced at the way he referred to me in the past tense, and said, "Not a lot."

Shuffling the cards, he asked, "What kind of programs did you watch? Soap operas?"

"No," I snapped. "I hate soap operas. Talk about a waste of time."

"I'm sorry, Nicole. I just assumed since you were a woman, you'd watch those types of programs."

"You shouldn't assume things about people."

"No?"

"No. You don't buy a book based solely on the cover, do you?"

He nodded. "You're right, Nicole. I'm sorry. It's just that I've known a lot of women who watched that type of thing."

"Was one of them your wife?"

Quickly, he stood, reached across the table, and slapped me hard, bringing tears to my eyes. I'd never been slapped before. It hurt like hell. It felt like dozens of pins stinging my face.

I know he saw the shock on my face as I rubbed my left cheek with my free hand.

"I'm sorry, Nicole. I shouldn't have done that," he said as he sat down in his chair again.

For a while, all I could do was look at him, shocked. I shouldn't be surprised, of course. He was a psychopath. I should be expecting anything at any time. But I hadn't seen that coming.

"I'm sorry. Let's just forget that ever happened, shall we? It's your turn," he said, indicating the cards.

"You can kiss my ass if you think I'm going to play with you after that."

"Nicole, please."

"No. I'm not in the mood to play cards anymore." I tried to cross my arms over my chest in a childish manner, but with my right arm shackled to the underside of the table, I could only cross my left arm. That probably looked at least half as stupid as it felt, so I relaxed my left arm, letting my hand fall to my lap limply.

Maybe I was crazy for talking back to him the way I was. I know he liked it when I did, but I also knew there was a very thin line that I couldn't see but knew I didn't want to cross. It would take him from amused by me to furious at me in the blink of an eye. But I didn't care at the moment. I was angry.

I didn't talk to him much the rest of the day. I watched as he cleaned the house, but if he looked my way, I averted my eyes. Eye contact provoked conversation and I wasn't in the mood for that.

While he cleaned, I pulled on my hand, trying desperately to free myself of the metal handcuff. I tried to bend my thumb over far enough into my palm to make it smaller. It didn't work. I even spit on my wrist and rubbed it around under the cuff trying to create enough lubricant to allow my hand to slip through. It didn't work either.

In fact, the only thing I succeeded in doing was rubbing my wrist raw and making the bones in my hand hurt.

There would come a day, though, when the cuff would be just loose enough for my wrist to slide out. Then I would be free. And Ron would be dead.

# 12

$\mathbf{A}$ couple of days later, I was cuffed to the table while Ron was in the basement. He'd been down there for a while. I didn't know what he was doing and I didn't care. When he'd first gone down, I'd heard Melinda's screams, but they'd fallen silent some time ago.

Now, I just sat and waited.

Eventually, Ron came stomping up the stairs in a huff. I could tell he was angry by the sounds of his footsteps. They were heavy, quick, and purposeful. I didn't turn around. I didn't want to face him, afraid I would be the center of his anger.

Turns out, I didn't have to turn around to be the center of his anger. And if I had put half as much thought into it as I thought I had, I would've seen this coming.

I heard his footsteps approach me from behind. They stopped directly behind me. I caved and started to turn around to face him, but before I could, he had his right arm across my right shoulder, and with his hand, he held my jaw tightly. His left hand came up on my left side. Before I could register that he had something in his hand, he was forcing it into my mouth.

I tried to pull away from him, but I had nowhere to go. My right hand was bound to the underside of the table. He was behind me, and I was trapped in his arms.

To my surprise and his, I managed to keep my teeth tightly together for a full minute. But no more than that. He stuffed his dirty, meaty fingers into my mouth and pried open my jaw. With his left hand, he managed to cram in a handful of the stuff he held, which I now knew to be the rotten dog food I'd so cleverly hidden from him.

He'd found it. He must've been down there cleaning and lifted the mattress. So as it turns out, I wasn't quite the genius I thought I was.

I was more afraid than I had been so far. Even more afraid than I'd been as I'd watched him hack Stephanie into pieces. I knew that he was angry. Not just angry, but directly angry at me, with me, for lying to him. I didn't even want to imagine the kind of punishment he had for something like this.

"Eat it, you stupid bitch," he said as he continued cramming wads of rotten dog food in my mouth. Some pieces were still hard and crumbled as they scraped across my teeth. But other pieces had gone soft in their decay and fell softly into my mouth, threatening to slide down my throat. It was a battle to keep any from going down.

I only had one free hand and I used it to alternately beat him in the face and pull at his arms. It was becoming increasingly difficult to breathe with my mouth and throat full of the foul kibble. I was trying to keep it all in my mouth so when he let go, I could spit it all in his face.

"You think you can lie to me and get away with it?" he screamed in my ear. "Eat it!"

I began to cough and choke. He stopped shoving more food in, but refused to allow any out. He cupped his left hand, which was still covered in dog food crumbs, over my mouth and bloated cheeks. With his right hand, he lifted up on my jaw, tilting my head back against his chest where I could feel his furiously pounding heart beating against his ribs, adding to the pounding I already had in my head.

"Eat it, bitch, or I'll snap your neck and then shove it down your throat while your heart still beats."

Trying not to choke, I swallowed what was in my throat, some of the pieces scratching as they went. It took a few swallows to get it down, but I finally managed. Then, I chewed what was in my mouth. He didn't give me any slack to chew, so I had to grind the bits of food against my teeth with my tongue to get it small enough to swallow. And worse, I could only breathe through my nose which meant I could smell. And taste. To say that it was a struggle to keep from puking was like saying that it was warm in Death Valley. A total understatement.

When he was satisfied that I'd swallowed enough of the vile stuff, he let go of my mouth and jaw. Just as I began to relax a little, he put a hand on the back of my head and shoved my face down onto the table hard enough to rattle my teeth and blur my vision. I'd managed to turn my head slightly to the left, making my cheek cushion the blow and avoiding a certain broken nose. I had not been able to keep from biting the inside of my jaw, however. The metallic taste of the blood was welcoming, as it masked the putrid taste of rotten dog food.

He leaned down and spoke directly into my ear loudly. "If you ever, ever, lie to me again, I'll bring your family here and make you watch as I slowly kill them. Do you understand me?"

I tried to nod, but his hand had my face pinned tightly against the table, so instead I said, "Yes," in a weak and defeated voice.

He let go of my head and stomped back downstairs. To the sound of his fading footsteps, I vomited. I threw up all the dog food, spilling it onto the kitchen floor. When I saw the maggots writhing around in it, I vomited again.

Using the back of my hand and the tail of my shirt, I wiped my face and mouth free of as much of the gross stuff as I could. Still, I could smell it. To expel as much of the smell as I could, I blew my nose into the tail of my shirt. It helped, but I still ended up breathing through only my mouth for the rest of the day.

Also for the rest of the day, I didn't speak to Ron or look at him. He didn't speak to me either.

When he finally allowed me to use the restroom, I saw myself in the mirror. I had bits of dog food in my hair. My face was bruised on the right side, where he'd slammed it against the table.

I didn't give a damn what he said. I stayed in the bathroom until I'd cleaned myself up a bit.

I brushed my teeth twice. I ran the sink full of icy water and plunged my face into it. I considered leaving it there and drawing a deep breath. It shouldn't take long to drown. The only problem would be my body working against me, fighting for life. I wasn't sure I could overcome the will to live. And as Mason popped forward in my mind, I knew I couldn't. His adorable little face was enough to make me pull my face from the sink and suck in a deep breath of air instead of water.

So what? What was the worst thing that had happened to me really? He'd shoved rotten dog food down my throat? Left me hungry in the basement? Left me without water for days? Made me piss the bed? Hacked up the body of a woman he'd killed only feet from me? Gave me a slap and some bruises? That wasn't so bad. I could handle that. I had to. For Mason. And Wade.

I walked out of the bathroom with my head held high, though I still wasn't in the mood to talk to Ron.

He seemed to have forgiven me. He talked to me as though nothing had happened. He made our dinner, and we ate as usual. We had drinks after dinner while playing cards. I said little to him, but he made more than enough conversation all by himself.

Shortly after we'd finished dinner, I began to feel groggy. It became a battle to keep my eyes open. I'd only had two drinks, so I knew that wasn't the problem. When the cards became blurry, I put my hand on the table and rested my head on it, thinking I'd just lay there for a minute until the feeling had passed.

Right before the blackness overcame me, I remembered the last time this had happened. It was a repeat performance of the last time I'd made him angry with me.

He pretended he was over it, made us dinner and drinks, and I became sleepy. When I woke, I was in...Oh no. I knew as I fell into a deep sleep what I would find when I awoke.

\*\*\*

Just as I suspected, I woke in the basement. Only this time, I wasn't on the mattress and cuffed to the pipe. I soon wished I was, though.

With my head pounding, I opened my eyes and surveyed the room around me.

Melinda was still spread out on the floor as she'd been the last time I'd seen her, but she didn't look as good as she had then. Her hair was filthy and caked with blood. Her skin was covered in dirt and bruises. Her wrists and ankles were raw and bloody from struggling against the restraints. And worse still, the fight had gone out of her. There wasn't even any left in her eyes.

I sat in a chair, hands cuffed behind my back and around the vertical beam not far from Melinda. I was only a few inches away from her right foot. She didn't appear to be awake, but at least she wasn't dead.

"Melinda," I said with a dry throat.

She didn't respond.

Once more, I said, "Melinda."

"She doesn't seem to be willing to talk to you, Nicole," said Ron behind me. I hadn't heard him come down the stairs, so he must've been back there silently waiting for me to wake up.

I was terrified of anything he may have planned for us, but I had to keep my wits about me, and more importantly, keep him liking me before I ended up like Melinda.

Slowly, Ron walked around me and stood on the opposite side of Melinda, in a position where he could see us both.

"Nicole, I've given much thought as to what your punishment should be. You have no idea how angry it makes me that you would lie to me like that," he said, his voice starting to boom. He closed his eyes and took a few deep breaths to calm down. Then, he continued. "I thought about putting you back down here on the mattress that you hated so much. But I felt that just wasn't going to teach you anything. After all, it didn't teach you anything the last time. So then I asked myself what would be worse than that? Do you know what I decided?"

I shook my head.

"I'm sure if you thought about it long enough, you'd know. Go ahead. Guess."

"Sorry, Ron. I'm afraid I left my crystal ball in my other pants, and I'm no mind-reader," I said, hoping to remind him that he liked me.

He smiled, but it was faint. "I've decided that as your punishment, I'm not going to punish you."

"Good. I agree with that."

"I'm going to punish her."

"What?"

"Yes, I'm going to make you watch as I punish Melinda for the things you've done. Maybe that will teach you what the mattress cannot."

"No, just put me back on the mattress. You know how much I hate it. Isn't that punishment enough?" I said quickly, trying to talk him out of hurting poor Melinda, who'd clearly been going through enough punishment already.

He smiled broadly. "I knew this would work."

I watched as he walked across the room and retrieved some items from the cabinet above the utility sink. He returned quickly to Melinda's left side, where he knelt facing me, in a position for me to watch. How very thoughtful of him.

Slapping her face, he said, "Melinda. Melinda wake up. There's someone here to see you."

Melinda's head slowly rolled from side to side, and she began to moan. She said something, but I couldn't make it out. It was probably her husband's name, thinking he'd come to rescue her. I myself had woken up many times uttering Wade's name, having dreamt that he'd shown up and busted down the door, killed Ron, and rescued me.

Using the cattle prod he'd brought from the cabinet, Ron shocked her awake with a scream.

"There," he said. "I don't want you to miss a thing. Now look who's came to see you." He pointed at me with the cattle prod, and Melinda's head slowly turned my way.

I expected to see hope in her eyes, or fear. I would've been happy to see any emotion at all, any sign of life. What I saw instead was nothing. She had dead eyes. Just as Stephanie had.

"Nicole has been a very bad girl, Melinda. And we've decided that as her punishment, she will watch me punish you. How does that sound to you?"

She groaned what I thought was a no and tried to shake her head, but it was so slow, it appeared her head was just lolling back and forth.

"I didn't agree to that," I said. I wanted to make sure she knew this hadn't been my idea, though deep down, I knew that it wouldn't matter what she knew. The hours, possibly the minutes, of her life was ticking down to zero. It was only a matter of time until he killed her, and then it wouldn't matter if she knew that I wasn't a part of his sick and twisted punishment or not. But I had to tell her. I had to know that she knew.

"Really?" Ron asked. "Are you saying you'll trade places with her? Would you like me to tie her to the chair and put you in her place?"

My heart raced. This was one of those moments in life that no one ever thinks is going to happen to them. And when thinking about what if it did happen, they always thought they would do the noble and honorable thing. And here it was, all laid out before me, unfolding both in slow motion and at the speed of light.

I said nothing. I felt horrible about it, but I couldn't volunteer to trade places with her. I just couldn't. I tried to rationalize it by thinking that she was a used-up prostitute whose husband urged her to sell her body. Looking at her arms, I could see she was a heavy drug user. Probably an alcoholic. She was middle-aged. Living the life she was living, she surely only had a few more years ahead of her. If she had any kids, they were probably grown. Unlike me, whose child was only a year old, and who hadn't even lived to see the end of her twenties. If it had to be one of us, it should be her.

But she was still a human, still a person with feelings and a family. And she would be receiving torture for things I'd done. That just wasn't fair.

It also wasn't fair that I was here. In this situation, in this moment, I had to choose my life over hers. This wasn't the time to be a hero and throw myself in front of a speeding train to save her. I had to save myself. Not for me as much as for my little Mason with his little brand new teeth and his wobbly newfound walk.

So I said nothing.

"That's what I thought," Ron said.

In all the years to come, assuming I survived, I would hear those words echo in my mind. *That's what I thought.* But the words weren't going to be what would haunt me. What would haunt me would be the look on Melinda's face when she realized that I wasn't going to trade places with her. If a soul could shatter into a million little pieces, hers just had. And if a heart could snap in half and drain the life juice out of a person, mine just had. If I lived a thousand years, I'd never forget the look on her face or the way I felt about myself in that moment. But even knowing all these things, I still couldn't bring myself to trade places with her. Had I not been a mother, maybe. But I was. And I just couldn't do it.

Ron laid an old leather tool belt on the floor beside him. From it, he pulled a hammer and a chisel. Still squatted, he moved toward her left hand.

"Nicole, make sure you watch this. Melinda, this is going to hurt a bit, I'm afraid."

Situating himself so that I could see his every move, he put one foot on her forearm and pressed down, paralyzing the muscles and tendons in her forearm and hand, making it impossible for her to move her fingers. He put the chisel against her skin and beat it one hard time with the hammer. That's all it took to cut off her finger.

As she screamed and howled through a hoarse throat, Ron picked up the finger and showed me. Her thin gold wedding band was still attached. He laid it on the tool belt and returned the tools to their place.

"Tell Nicole how much you enjoy taking her punishment," he told Melinda.

In between screams, she shouted, "I hate you, bitch!"

Through my tears, I said, "I'm sorry. I'm so sorry."

"Go to hell," she screamed to me. To Ron, she begged, "Please stop. Pleasepleaseplease stop."

Of course he didn't.

He pulled a knife from the tool belt. I guessed the blade to be about eight inches long. It was big. He put it to Melinda's belly, and I could only watch as she began to thrash around as much as possible while alternately begging him to stop and screaming.

"Since this is for Nicole, I thought we'd carve her name onto your flesh. What do you think of that, Melinda?"

"No," she screamed. "Please no! Please!"

As Ron began to carve into Melinda's skin, making a large N as slowly as he could, I began to beg him to stop. Melinda's and my pleas mingled together.

"I guess you should just be happy that her name isn't Marguerite," he joked as he continued slicing her.

As the blood spilled off her belly and slowly ran across the floor toward the drain, I cried harder than I had since he'd brought me here. Her pain was because of me. And if I'd been a stronger person, a better person, I would've switched places with her. But I couldn't. All I could do was watch and cry and beg him to stop.

"There," he said when he'd spelled out my name in big letters across her stretch marked belly. "Now you can always remember this day, and your good friend Nicole."

She continued to scream, though her voice was going. It broke often, cutting out completely at times.

Ron stood with his tools and turned to walk away from her. But he quickly turned back and stuck the cattle prod to one of the open cuts on her belly. She howled and screamed through clenched teeth as her body spasmed, and then suddenly, there was nothing else.

Afraid she was dead, I focused on her face and chest. She was still very much alive. But her voice was gone. She was still screaming her head off, but no sound came from her.

Ron chuckled and walked away. He returned everything to its place and walked over to me.

"I'm going upstairs. I'll come retrieve you later. Enjoy your time with Melinda. Had her voice not given out on her, I'm sure she would've had plenty to say to you." He smiled and walked up the stairs, leaving me in the basement, crying and laden with guilt.

# 13

I cried nearly the entire time I was in the basement. I couldn't help it. The guilt was heavy, though I tried to tell myself that he was torturing her anyway, and he would've surely done those things to her even without me as a reason. The only reason he said it was my fault was to torture me too. He liked me enough to not want to torture me physically, but not enough keep him from torturing me mentally, emotionally, and psychologically. I knew this really wasn't my fault, but I still felt horrible.

Some time later, Ron returned. As he removed the cuff from my left wrist and helped me to my feet, he asked, "Are you glad to see me?"

"Yes," I said, though the answer was both yes and no. I was glad to be leaving the basement, but I was never glad to see him.

"Good. I thought you might be." He kissed my cheek softly and led me up the stairs. "I made you some scrambled eggs and bacon and toast."

Confused, I asked, "It's morning?"

"Of course."

"You left me down there all night?"

"Yes. It doesn't seem like it, does it? Time flies when you're having fun."

The son of a bitch had left me down there all night. No wonder I was tired and my back was stiff.

Even though he sometimes slipped something into my food to knock me out so he could take me to the basement, I was looking forward to eating a good breakfast. He'd only done it a couple times so far, and only after I'd angered him. I was starving and he was a good cook. As I'd done nothing wrong, I didn't think he'd drug me again so soon.

I sat in the usual chair as he locked the cuff to the underside of the table. I yawned, and immediately felt guilty about doing so. Melinda had gone through all that, and I was yawning and upset because he'd left me in the basement all night. I was selfish.

I was wiping my swollen eyes with my hand when he brought my plate. He set it down in front of me, went to the other side of the table, and took his seat.

With the spoon in my hand, I scooped up a wad of scrambled eggs and put them in my mouth. As always, they were delicious. I put another scoop in my mouth and looked around at the other food on my plate. The bacon looked perfect. The toast had the right amount of butter melted into it. But then I saw something else, something that nearly made me vomit.

I stopped chewing immediately and stared at it. Ron must've been watching me.

"I think that's appropriate, don't you?"

I shook my head, afraid that if I opened my mouth to speak, I'd puke.

"You don't have to eat it. It's just a little reminder."

Forcing myself to swallow the mouthful of eggs, I said, "What's it supposed to remind me of, Ron? The kind of person you are?"

"No. It's to remind you to be a good girl."

"How can I eat with that on my plate?"

"It's not touching any food. It's just there for you to see. You don't have to touch it or eat it. Just see it."

"I don't know if I can eat with it there. It's gross. Can't you just put it on the table or something? Does it have to be on my plate?"

"Yes, Nicole. It does," he said sharply. "How else will you learn?" He softened his voice and said, "Think of it as Melinda giving you the finger." He laughed.

I didn't.

How the hell was I supposed to eat with a severed finger on my plate, nestled between the eggs and the bacon? How could I even have an appetite when she'd lost that finger because of me? I hated him and I hated myself.

I dropped the spoon. It fell to the plate, clanking against the wedding band on the finger.

"You're not finished, are you? You've hardly eaten any-thing."

"I'm not very hungry."

"You were until you saw the reminder. Is that what's wrong?"

"Yeah. It's disgusting. I can't eat with that there, especially knowing it's my fault."

He smiled and nodded. "Then it's working perfectly. I want you to eat, don't get me wrong. But I want you to learn. Yes, this lesson has already taught you so much more than just being left on an old mattress did. I don't see that we'll have any more problems, do you?"

I shook my head.

I didn't eat anymore at breakfast. I just couldn't. But at lunch, it was on the plate. At supper, it was on the plate. The next morning, there it was, sitting beside my waffles. At lunch, it was lying beside my sandwich. At dinner, it was beside the pot roast on my plate. Every meal for the next few days was garnished with Melinda's severed finger. It was starting to smell. Even over the mouth-watering aromas of the food, I could detect the stench of decay rising from the plate. Just as my stomach growled from the anticipation of the food, it flip-flopped at the smell and sight of the finger.

This went on for days. Ron brought me a hearty plate of food containing a rotting finger, and each time, he took it away untouched. By the seventh day, I was absolutely starving. I had to eat something. As Ron sat across from me eating as if nothing was wrong, I managed to talk myself into eating without looking at the finger or eating anything on the same side of the plate as the finger. If I only ate the food on the opposite side of the plate, that would be okay. Well, not okay, but better than eating the food near the rotting digit, and certainly better than starving.

That method worked for a couple of days, but Ron soon caught on to what I was doing. Then, he started serving my plates to me with the finger in the middle of the food. For a few days, I didn't eat. But when the hunger pains returned, I started eating the food from the edges of the plate. Anything that wasn't close to the finger, I ate.

Finally, sometime after my next menstrual cycle, Ron quit putting the finger on my plate altogether. When I first didn't see the appendage among my food, I worried that he'd cooked it and was serving it to me. I hesitated at dinner the first night without it, afraid to eat the food. I couldn't shake the thought that chopped up inside the meat loaf was what was left of the flesh from the finger.

Ron saw my hesitation and explained himself. "The skin was rotting off the bone, and I don't want you to accidentally eat any of it and get sick. When the skin is completely rotted away, I may return the bones to your plate, but I don't think that'll be necessary. I truly believe you've learned your lesson. Am I wrong, Nicole?"

I shook my head, disgusted that he still had the finger. I briefly wondered where he was keeping it. Up until now, he'd kept it in a bag in the freezer, taking it out for each meal, returning it when the meal was done. I had no doubt that it was there now, as he spoke, and I wondered how long he would leave it in there.

It wasn't long after he stopped putting her finger on my plate that Melinda died.

Ron had come to my room that night and asked me if I was ready to have him. I told him I still wasn't ready, which of course made him angry. I heard him storm down the steps to the basement, and I didn't hear him return until the sun shone through the windows the next morning. He dragged himself into my room to tell me that she'd died. Judging by the way he looked that morning as he stood beside the bed, hair disheveled, eyes wild, clothes filthy and bloody, I had no doubt that he'd raped her and killed her, just as he had Stephanie. And just as with Stephanie, it was all because I wouldn't have sex with him.

The guilt was heavier after that. It was my fault. Everything that had happened to her was my fault. It was even my fault that she was here. Had I not made him angry, he might not have killed Stephanie. Then, he wouldn't have been at the bar the night he ran into Melinda. He wouldn't have brought her home with him, and she wouldn't have been here to endure the torture that he inflicted upon her in my name. All. My. Fault.

As I watched him bring Melinda out of the basement one bag at a time, I knew what I had to do.

I spent a few days trying to talk myself into letting him have me in the way that he wanted, hoping that maybe he wouldn't bring another girl to this house and torture her the way he had the others. But it was too late. By the time I worked up the nerve to tell him that he could have me in that way, he had already brought another girl to the house.

# 14

He woke me one morning, rushing me to hurry and get ready. I quickly worked through my morning routine wondering what had him in such a fuss.

When he led me down the basement steps I started to think I didn't want to know. And when I saw her lying there where the others had been, naked and spread open for all to see, I wished I didn't know.

I gasped. If Ron heard, he ignored it.

"Nicole, this is Crystal. Crystal, Nicole." As he pushed me into the chair and pulled my arms behind me, cuffing me to the vertical beam, I took a good look at Crystal. I knew she'd never look this way again.

If she was twenty years old, I'd be surprised. My guess was more like eighteen, maybe even younger than that. She had black hair with white streaks bleached into it. She had many piercings. I saw two in her lower lip, two in one eyebrow and four in the other, and several in her right ear. I couldn't see her left ear, but I assumed it contained as many or more. Her belly button was pierced, as well as her nipples and her crotch.

She had several tattoos here and there on her body. Each ankle had something on it, but I couldn't make out what either was because the restraints covered most of them. Above her privates where her pubic hair would've been if she'd had any was the face of a black cat. It could've been a panther. It was hard to tell in the dim lighting, but I knew for sure it was a black cat. Above each of her breasts was a black paw print, probably in keeping with the cat theme. On the side of her neck was what looked like a name. From this distance and angle, I couldn't read it. Though I couldn't see her back side, I was sure she had a tramp stamp, a tattoo above her butt. Oddly and inappropriately, I wondered what it was.

She was a very pretty girl, but judging her from what I saw before me now, I bet she was a wild one.

I also noticed something that Ron probably hadn't. She had a bump. A baby bump. She was slender and the bump was slight, but I noticed it.

I looked to Ron, but he was standing over her looking at her face. He didn't appear to have noticed her bump. I certainly didn't want to bring it up. But I also didn't want him to do anything to hurt the baby. I wondered if he would let her go if he knew she was pregnant. Did he have any morals whatsoever? Did even madmen have a line they wouldn't cross? I doubted it, and I kept my mouth shut.

"Look at you," he said to her. "How could you do this to your body?" He knelt down beside her. "Your beautiful, young, soft body." He lightly ran the back of his hand up her thigh and side. Just before he touched her breast, he looked at me. "Does this bother you, Nicole?"

I didn't know what to say so I said nothing.

"Does it bother you when I touch her this way?" he asked as he caressed her left breast with his right hand.

I looked at her face. She was crying. If this made her cry, she was in trouble because this was nothing compared to what was going to happen to her.

"Nicole, do you feel any jealousy?"

Unsure of what to say but knowing I had to say something, I said, "A little." I was afraid that if I said no, he'd get angry and harm her. I was also afraid that if I said yes, he'd rape her to make me more jealous.

He nodded. "I thought so."

He got on his knees and leaned over her, kissing her breast. The unsettling part of the whole thing wasn't that she was tied up or that we were both being held against our will. It was that while he licked her nipples, he stared at me. Even as he ran his left hand down her belly and settled between her legs, he kept eye contact with me. Just as he had when he'd been raping Stephanie's corpse.

In my peripheral vision, I saw his hand moving between her legs, slowly at first, then gaining speed. His mouth went from licking and kissing her nipple to biting it, softly at first, then harder and harder.

She went from whimpering and weeping silently to crying openly. Soon, she'd move on to screaming. They always did.

As he kept eye contact with me, he began to get really rough with her. The more she cried and struggled, the harder he bit her, and the harder his hand went at her crotch.

When the screams started suddenly, I looked down at his hand and saw him pulling it out of her. The sight of blood made me first think he'd caused enough harm to make her lose the baby. But after a while, I realized it wasn't enough blood for that, and that the only person he had hurt was her. He shoved his hand into her again, all the way up to his wrist, and back out.

Able to only imagine what kind of pain that brought, I squeezed my legs together and winced. That poor girl.

"What about now, Nicole?" he asked.

I snapped my eyes from his hand up to his face, which hovered only an inch or two above her bleeding breast.

"Are you jealous now? Would you like to trade places with her?"

"No," I said quickly. I immediately felt guilty. She was pregnant. I should offer to take her place. And if I knew for a fact that he'd let her go, I would. But I had a feeling that even if I took her place, he'd kill her.

I squeezed my eyes shut tight for a moment and reminded myself that I had a baby of my own I had to think about. As Mason's face floated behind my eyelids, I felt better about what I'd said. As unfair as it was to judge her this way, I told myself that she wouldn't

94

make a good mother anyway. I was hoping she would escape with her life and that of her unborn child, but if she didn't, then it was probably for the best.

Maybe now I'd be able to sleep at night.

When I opened my eyes, I was surprised to find Ron's face right in front of mine. He was kneeling in front of me. I drew back a bit, startled.

"Nicole," he said softly. "It makes me happy to know that seeing me touch another woman makes you jealous. It shows me that you care about me. Knowing this, I still don't understand why you won't have me."

He reached up and touched my face. That alone was bad, but this time it was worse. He touched me with the hand that had her blood on it. Some of her blood was on his chin as well. He leaned in and kissed my neck. It was all I could do to keep from cringing.

Behind him, she cried.

"You do things to me, Nicole. Things like sleep naked across the hall from me, teasing me. You let me touch you and kiss you, but you turn me away night after night. Why do you torment me so?" he asked as he nuzzled my neck and ran his bloody hand through my hair.

"You make me sleep naked, Ron. Remember?"

"Yes. Yes, I remember. You know I sleep naked too. Just waiting for the night you call out my name, summoning me to come to you. I'll be there in a flash, you know."

And in the blink of an eye, he changed. He went from cooing words of affection to me to yelling.

He stood up quickly and paced around Crystal's nude body, arms flailing and eyes wide. And penis erect, bulging at the front of his slacks.

No. I'd seen this play out before. I knew what he was getting ready to do. I had to stop him. If I didn't at least try, I might as well be down on the floor beside him, raping her right along with him.

"Ron, I may be ready to have you."

"Oh is that so?" he asked in a snotty tone without breaking his pace.

"Yes. I was going to tell you today. I've given it a lot of thought, and I believe I'm ready."

He shot a glance my way but didn't stop pacing. "Why? Why now?"

"I've spent more time with you and feel that I know you better now." The next part was a tough one to say, but after glancing at Crystal, I managed. "I like you now."

He stopped pacing and looked at me. "You mean you didn't like me before?"

Shit. No matter what I said with him, it was wrong. It was always the wrong thing to say and the wrong time to say it.

"I've always kind of liked you," I stammered. "But now I like you more. I like you enough to have you."

He shook his head.

"It's true. I really do want you." I was starting to sound like I meant it. I hoped he believed me.

Then, he smiled. He stepped closer to me. "You want me?"

"Yes."

He unfastened his khaki slacks and pulled them and his underwear down until all of his maleness was exposed. I watched as he walked toward me. My heart was beating furiously. This was it. I'd made it a long time, but now it was going to happen.

He stopped in front of me. I waited for him to remove the handcuffs. Surely, he would put me on the floor or the mattress, or maybe even make me stand up and turn around, giving me a chance at least to get away. But he didn't.

He put his hand on the back of my head and pulled it toward his exposed crotch as he stepped closer to me.

"You bite me, Nicole, and I'll cut off more than just her finger. Do you understand?"

Slowly, I nodded. I tried to talk myself into this. I didn't want to do it. Not even a little bit. But it was clear that I had to. It would prevent her from suffering any more than she already was. I felt I owed her that much after having thrown her under the bus as much as I felt I had.

I opened my mouth and began the disgusting task at hand, doing my best to forget that what was now in my mouth had been inside a dead woman, and reminding myself of why I couldn't bite him. I wanted to bite the damn thing off and watch him bleed to death, but I knew that wouldn't happen. That would be suicide for me and nothing more than an inconvenient and embarrassing trip to the emergency room for him.

After several minutes which felt like hours, and nearly vomiting twice, he pulled himself away from me. I thought this would be the time when he'd release me and have his way. But that's not what he did.

He turned and walked over to Crystal. He dropped to his knees between her legs. Looking over at me, he said, "I want you to watch this, Nicole. I think watching me with her will make you jealous enough to love me." He smiled and began to rape her.

\*\*\*

That was our routine for the next couple of weeks. After break-fast, he would make me go down to the basement with him and watch as he raped her. Then, after he stripped me naked and strapped me to the bed at night, I could see that he was once again aroused. After he left my room, I heard him going down the steps to the base-ment, where I was certain that he raped her again. That was twice a day, nearly every day. That poor girl.

Since he made me go down with him every day, I watched her deteriorate before my eyes. She became thin. Her skin lost its glow, and even the pregnancy couldn't bring it back.

When I'd first saw her, I'd thought she would've been tough, a fighter. I'd thought she would be a mouthy girl who fought until the end. But I was wrong. She was quiet. Instead of screaming and curs-ing at him the way Melinda had, Crystal cried and whimpered. She begged sometimes, but always quietly.

I struggled to understand Ron. I'd finally offered myself to him, but instead of taking me, he chose to make me watch as he raped Crystal. I just couldn't understand him.

The only thing that made any sort of sense was if he really be-lieved that I wanted him and thought that by making me watch him with her, it was a punishment to me for making him wait so long. It was crazy to a normal person, but to a psycho like Ron, it would make perfect sense.

I didn't want to watch him with her, though not for the reason he hoped. I didn't want to watch two regular people have sex, and I sure as hell didn't want to watch a man rape a pregnant young woman.

That's why I looked away. Just one time. And that was all it took.

I'd turned my head toward the mattress in the corner. I just couldn't watch anymore. I heard Ron shout my name. When I looked back at him, he ordered me to keep watching. Then he began to strangle Crystal. With his big hands around her slender neck, he choked her until he'd finished with her, releasing his grip just before she passed out each time.

To keep him from causing her more harm similar to or worse than that, I always made myself watch. I focused on what I could see of his face, though, still trying to figure out what he was thinking.

This is the way things went until after my next period. Since I had no other method of keeping track of time, I had to use my menstrual cycle. This happened right after my period because that's when Ron noticed that Crystal wasn't having periods.

Ron and I were sitting at the table after dinner playing cards and having drinks. After being silent for a long time, he finally asked what I hoped he never would.

"Why do you suppose Crystal doesn't have periods?"

With no time to weigh my words, I said, "Well, maybe she hasn't started her period yet."

I felt him stare at me as I sorted through the cards in my hand. "Is that possible?"

Shrugging it off as if it were no big deal, I said, "It's possible. Some girls start really young, some really late, and some never start at all."

He was silent a few more minutes. Then, "Have you not noticed her belly, Nicole?"

"Her belly?" I asked, trying to sound as though I had no idea what he was talking about.

"Yes, her belly. She has a noticeable protrusion from her midsection. Coupled with her lack of menstrual cycles, I can't help but wonder if the girl's pregnant." Though he'd said it, it felt more like a question.

"I guess it's possible," I said lightly. I didn't want him to know she was pregnant. I wasn't sure if it would be better or worse if he knew, but I had to assume it would be worse. I suppose I'd been trying to keep him from knowing with the hopes that I could find a way out and save her before he knew she was with child.

"Nicole, I think you know more than you let on."

"How could I know anything? I'm not a doctor. I've never even touched her. How would I know?"

"You're a woman."

"So that makes me a psychic?"

"You can detect changes in another woman's body."

"Yeah, if I'd known her before maybe I could. How do I know that she just doesn't have an addiction to Oreos?"

He didn't chuckle as I expected him to. "That's not an Oreo belly, Nicole, and you know that. It's not a chip belly, or an ice cream belly, or even a beer belly. That is a baby belly. And I believe you know that."

"But I don't know that."

"Have you noticed it?"

"Yeah." I saw no reason to lie about that.

"And you didn't bring it my attention?" he asked as he discarded his last card.

After adding up my score and telling him, I said, "You're closer to her than me. You're on top of her every day. I figured you'd know."

"Oh. That's what this is about," he said as if he'd just figured everything out. "You hate that I'm with her and not you."

"That's not really true." In a way, it was. I hated that he was raping a pregnant girl. It wasn't that I wanted him to myself.

"Not really true? So it is somewhat true?"

"Somewhat."

Now he chuckled as he shuffled. "Would it make you feel better if I stopped being with her and began being with you?"

I swallowed the bile that rose in the back of my throat at the thought of him touching me. "Yes."

He smiled and nodded. "Very well then. I suppose that's the way it will be. Although, Crystal may be disappointed at the lack of a lover."

"I somehow don't think she'll mind," I snapped.

He laughed. "There's my girl."

I hated that he referred to me as his girl, but it beat not being his girl. I'd seen first-hand what happened to girls that weren't his.

"The book is coming along nicely. You've been a bigger help than you could imagine. And Crystal has made a wonderful addition."

"You put her in there too?"

"Of course. They're all in it." He smiled and looked at me over his cards, brows pulled together. "Does that make you jealous?"

"No."

"Are you sure?"

I thought for a minute, trying to make sure that no was the right answer. "No, I'm not jealous. I mean, I'm the star of the book, right?" He nodded. "I'm just surprised to hear that they're in it too."

"I've changed their names, of course, but I had to add them. It makes the story more exciting. Now there are love triangles."

"Between who?"

"Nicole, don't act as if you don't know. Just as in life, things are more interesting when there's jealousy. Sex with Crystal is more exciting if you're jealous. And I'm sure she'll be jealous when she finds out that I won't be with her anymore because I'm with you. It's better."

"What's going to happen when the book is finished?"

"I'm going to find a publisher and become a best-selling author." He smiled.

"I mean with me. What about me?"

"I'm not sure yet, Nicole. You've been a good girl for the most part. If you continue to be a good girl, I may let you go. However, that may not be in my best interest. You could run to the authorities. How will I become a best-selling author if I'm in prison?"

"I wouldn't tell," I said. Sadly, I actually thought about keeping my silence if he'd only let me go.

"We'll see."

And that was it for the conversation about my release.

Unfortunately, it wasn't the end of the conversation about Crystal's pregnancy.

# 15

Strapped to the chair, hands bound behind me, I watched as Ron slapped Crystal's cheeks to wake her. When her eyes opened, she tensed.

"Good morning," he said cheerfully.

"Please," she said.

"If you don't mind, Crystal, I'll talk. You only speak if I ask you a question. Does that sound okay to you?"

"No," she said.

"Are you a prostitute?"

"No."

"Are you a runaway?"

"No."

"Do you have a husband?"

"No."

"Do you have a boyfriend?"

"Yeah."

"What's his name?"

"Corey."

"Does Corey have a job?"

"No."

"Do you have a job?"

"No."

"Are you pregnant?"

"No."

He hesitated, and then asked again, "Are you pregnant?"

"No."

I gasped as he hit her in the belly with his fist. It wasn't as hard as he could've hit her, but it was hard enough to cause fetal damage, and possibly a miscarriage.

Crystal cried out.

"I'm going to ask you again, and it would be wise for you to answer me honestly. Do you hear me?"

She nodded.

"Are you pregnant?"

"Yes," she cried.

"Do you think it's wise to bring a child into the world when neither of you have a job? Do you plan to have the working people support you and boyfriend while you spit out child after child, none of which you can support? Do you?"

"No," she answered through tears.

"I don't either," he said. "Why didn't you tell me you were pregnant?"

She didn't answer immediately.

He patted her belly roughly, reminding her of what would happen if she didn't answer him. "Answer me."

"Would it have made a difference? Would you have left me on the street if you'd known?"

"I'm asking the questions here, Crystal. You just answer them. Why didn't you tell me?"

"I was afraid."

He smiled and said, "You should be."

He stood and stared down at her. "Do you and Corey have a good relationship?"

"Sort of."

"What does that mean? Does he hit you?"

"Yeah, sometimes."

"What else?"

"He...he cheats on me."

"Come on now, Crystal."

"What? He does."

"But don't you cheat on him too?"

"No."

"Crystal, don't lie to me. Would you like to ask Nicole what happens to girls who lie to me?"

He looked at me and I took that as my cue to speak, so I said, "Tell the truth, Crystal. Please."

She glanced at me quickly, and then looked back at Ron. "Once. I only did it once."

"If I only rape you once, does that mean it doesn't count? If I only cut off one of your fingers, does that make it okay since it was just the one time?"

She shook her head.

"You lied to me."

"I didn't lie."

"Well what do you call it?"

"I just didn't tell you something that was none of your business."

"Well withholding something is the same as lying, isn't it?"

"If that's the case, you lied to me too."

"What?" he asked with a little laugh.

"Yeah. You didn't tell me what you were going to do to me. You didn't tell me you were a fucking lunatic."

"Such language," he said. He threw his head up and looked at the ceiling. He sighed deeply. "Well, you did lie to me. Twice, technically. But I'll only charge you with the first one, the big one. Lying about your pregnancy is too big to let slide." To me, he asked, "What should we do with her?"

I had no idea what I should say. I said nothing, hoping he would move on and treat it as if it were a rhetorical question.

But he didn't.

"Nicole, what sort of punishment do you think fits the crime?"

Thinking stupidly that I could outsmart him, I said "Slap her around a little bit maybe."

"You can do better than that, Nicole."

I tried to think of something he could do to her that would cause the least amount of harm to the baby. Clearly, he wouldn't be satisfied with anything small. It would have to be big.

Unable to believe what I was getting ready to say, I opened my mouth and let the horrible words that were sure to haunt me all of my days fall from my tongue. "Maybe you could pull out her piercings."

He smiled at me and nodded. "That's my girl."

She looked at me like she wanted to kill me. I didn't blame her. At that moment, I very much wanted to die.

"Very good, Nicole. I don't think that'll be punishment enough, but it's a good start."

He bent down, hooked his finger in the two silver loops that hooked over Crystal's bottom lip, and yanked. She'd turned at the last second, trying to keep him from ripping them out of her flesh, but instead only making it worse.

Ron threw the lip rings to the floor behind him and grabbed the ones in her eyebrows. One by one, he ripped them out, taking no care whatsoever.

Tired of fighting with her, he put one knee on each side of her face, holding her head so she couldn't turn away from him. He pulled her earrings out one at a time. First came the scream, and then came the small ting of the metal on the concrete floor.

I couldn't see her face because he was blocking my view, but from the sounds, I could tell he was ripping out her tongue ring.

God forgive me. This was something else I'd always feel guilty about. It was once again my fault that an innocent woman was suffering.

He returned to the squatted position beside her and grabbed her belly button ring between his thumb and index finger. He looked at it closely, pulling it up slowly, until her skin was stretched. Then, he pulled a little harder, causing it to snap free, leaving blood where the ring had just been. Another ting as he tossed it to the floor.

"That leaves just one more, I believe," he said as he leaned down and grabbed the piercing that shined on her crotch. As he slowly pulled it the way he had her belly button, I cringed. He said, "I'm going to hate to see this one go." Then, he yanked it, causing her to scream.

I squeezed my legs closed and suffered through sympathy pains that in no way matched the pain she was going through.

"Did that hurt?"

"You know it did, you son of a bitch," she yelled through her tears.

"Well it hurt me when you lied to me."

"That's not the same and you know it," she wailed.

Walking over to the cabinet over the utility sink, he said, "I know a great many things, Crystal. But there are still a great many things I don't know. For example," he said as he returned with the tool belt. "I don't know why a beautiful young woman such as you would want to ruin her body with this hideous graffiti." He squatted and pulled the knife from the tool belt. It was the same knife he'd used to carve my name into Melinda's belly.

My stomach knotted and my skin crawled. I squeezed my eyes shut tightly—but I dared only do it briefly—and for the billionth time since the day he'd brought me here, screamed in my head to wake up. This had to be a nightmare. But when I opened my eyes, I sadly realized this wasn't my nightmare. It was Crystal's.

I watched as Ron straddled Crystal's chest. I saw her struggling to get away from him, and was saddened to know that she couldn't. With Ron blocking my view, I couldn't really see what he was doing, but I knew. And if I hadn't known, her screams would've told me.

I cried silently, sitting in the chair, hands cuffed around the beam behind me. I hated him. I hated being here. I hated having to witness the horrible things he did to these women. I hated knowing that this one was pregnant. This one, he should've left alone. But he didn't. Because he was a freaking psycho.

When the screams suddenly stopped, I held my breath. Had she died? Had he killed her? Was that what he was doing to her, slitting her throat?

But then he laid a piece of meat on the floor beside him. It was bloody, but I could clearly make out what was on it. A paw print.

He looked over his shoulder at me. "It isn't fun if she isn't awake." He laughed, and then he got up and ran upstairs. When he returned, he went by me so fast I couldn't see what he was holding. But when he used it, I knew.

The screams coming from Crystal now made all the ones before it sound like whispers. Her high-pitched screaming hurt my ears. But it was nothing compared to the pain she was feeling as Ron stood over her, pouring salt into the hole in her skin where her tattoo had been.

"There we go," he said, sitting the salt on the floor and kneeling. "It's much better when you're awake."

Her screams were so loud, I could barely hear him speak. And they continued for quite some time. I had no doubt that the salt was painful, but I had apparently underestimated how painful it was.

Ron grew annoyed by her constant screaming. He began to pace beside her, shooting her hateful glances from time to time.

Finally, he said to me, "I can see we're going to have to finish this later. Let's go upstairs for now."

As he led me up the stairs, I couldn't help but think of the way he'd said we would finish this later. I hated that he thought of me as part of his sick world. I didn't want to be a part of anything of his. I wanted to be home with my husband and son. I wanted to be in a world where Ron and others like him didn't exist.

We had lunch as we normally did. He'd made tuna salad sandwiches. If he ever considered giving up his career as a psychopath, he could easily become a chef. Even the simplest things he made were absolutely delicious (as long as there wasn't a rotting finger involved). Or maybe I just thought they were so good because I never knew which meal would be my last. Either way, I ate two sandwiches.

When we were finished, he said, "I'm going to do things a bit different today. I hope you don't mind."

"What do you mean?"

As he cleared away our plates, he said, "Normally, I work on my novel after I've put you to bed at night and before I wake you in the morning. But Crystal has given me so much to write, I need to get it down while it's still fresh in my mind."

"Okay," I said, unsure of how this was going to affect me.

"I'm wondering if I should gag you. I mean, if someone was to ring the doorbell, and you were to scream, things would get bad, wouldn't they?" He looked at me and considered whether I was trustworthy.

"I wouldn't scream, Ron."

After a moment of intense scrutiny, he said, "You probably wouldn't. But just in case, I'm going to leave the door to my bedroom open. If I hear anything from you that constitutes trying to gain attention from anyone other than myself, I'll cause a great deal of damage to our young friend in the basement. Do you understand?"

I nodded. It pissed me off that he always threatened me with harm to others.

"Very well. If you need me, you may loudly say my name. I should easily hear you." He kissed my forehead and left me sitting at the table while he retreated to his bedroom.

For the first few minutes, I tried to pull myself free from the handcuff.

For the next few minutes, I tried to pull the metal hook out of the underside of the table.

For the few minutes after that, I rested, having used up a lot of strength with all the pulling and tugging.

Then, I decided to do whatever exercises I could with one hand shackled so low. In my time with Ron, I'd noticed changes in my body. A weakening of muscles, especially in my right arm because it was always handcuffed to something. My legs were weaker too. There was going to come a time when I'd need to fight Ron or run away, and this was no shape in which to do either.

I stood and did some stretches. My muscles were weak from lack of use, and they were stiff. I knew I'd be sore tomorrow, so I tried not to push myself too hard. I didn't want Ron to know I was doing any exercises. I didn't know if it would make him angry, but there was no sense in poking the bear.

After managing to do some push-ups with my hands on the seat of the chair, I quietly slid the chair out of the way and laid on the floor. With my right hand shackled to the table and held up above me, I managed to do several sit-ups. Exercising made me feel better. It made me feel stronger and more in control.

When I'd finished exercising for the day, I sat in the chair.

I was thirsty now. When my breathing had returned to normal and I didn't think Ron could notice anything different, I called out to him. He didn't come the first time. Or the second time. On the third time, he came.

"What is it?"

"I'm very thirsty. Could you please get me a glass of ice water?"

"Sure." He poured me a glass and brought it to me. "It would be nice if I didn't have to restrain you, wouldn't it? Wouldn't it be wonderful if you could live here without me worrying you would try to get away?"

"Yes, Ron." It would be. Because then he could remove the handcuffs, go to his room, and I could get the hell out of here.

"Well, if that's all, I guess I'll get back to work. Call if you need anything else." Another kiss on the forehead, and he was gone.

Had he not been a psychopath, he would've surely made some lucky gal a great husband. If you left out the sadistic serial killer part of him, he was a great guy. He was clean and orderly. He was kind. He catered to the woman he loved. He was a great cook. He had high hopes for his career. He didn't plop down in front of the television for hours at a time. He enjoyed playing games and great conversation. His sexual stamina was impressive. And he was a handsome man. It's just that pesky habit of his where he raped, tortured, killed, and dismembered women that was a turn off.

I sat there for what felt like hours more, thinking, but trying not to.

It angered me that there were no clocks visible to me. The microwave was digital and had a clock, but it was always flashing twelve o'clock. The stove didn't have a clock. None hung on the walls, and Ron didn't wear a watch. I had no idea how he ever knew what time it was.

So I never knew the time, I never knew what day it was or what week it was or even what month it was. All I had to go on were my periods, which thankfully, came like clockwork. So I knew that I'd had three periods here so far. So I'd been here about four months. Damn. That was way too long. Of course, four minutes would've been too long also.

Even though I needed to pee, I didn't call for Ron. The more he wrote on that stupid book, the quicker this nightmare would end. Or so I hoped.

# 16

The next few days went the same way. We ate breakfast, he ran down and offered Crystal a fresh bowl of dog food, which he complained about her refusing to eat, and then he went to his bedroom to write while I secretly exercised at the table. I would yell to him when I got hungry and he would come and make us lunch, after which he returned to his room. The same thing happened for supper. I was hungry. I yelled for him. He made us dinner. Then, he retreated back to his room. We didn't even have drinks or play cards. Which was fine by me.

Except after a few days of that, I grew extremely bored. Just sitting at the kitchen table all day was mind-numbing. I hated it.

During dinner one night, I begged him for something to do while I sat at the table.

"Like what?"

"I don't know. Crossword puzzles, real puzzles, word searches, magazines, books, anything really. Just something to do other than sit here and stare at the floor."

"You could always try staring at the wall."

I looked at him and he laughed, clearly trying to be funny.

"You're hilarious," I said dryly.

"Come on, Nicole. Don't be so serious all the time. I'll see that you have something with which to occupy yourself tomorrow."

"Can I read your book?"

"I told you, not until it's finished."

"Not that one. The other one. The one you said bombed."

"I never said it bombed. Bombed is such a negative word. Why would want to read that one?"

I shrugged. "I don't know. Just to get a sense of your style." I was curious. I wanted a closer look to how his mind worked.

"I'll think about it."

I dropped the subject for the rest of the evening. I guess he felt bad for me because he actually stayed and played cards with me that evening after dinner. As much as I hated to admit it, it was better than nothing. I never would've thought that I'd find myself preferring the company of the sadistic over loneliness.

That night, as he shackled me to the headboard and hovered over my body, he smiled.

"Do you still want me?" he asked.

What the hell was I supposed to say to that? No, I did not want him to do anything except drop dead. But I couldn't tell him that.

I slowly nodded.

He kissed my neck gently while he caressed my breast with his hand. His light kisses on my neck gave me gooseflesh, which made my nipples hard under Ron's hand, which made Ron think I was enjoying his touch. It wasn't true, but that's what he thought.

"Oh, Nicole," he whispered breathlessly. "You really do want me."

Damn the goose bumps.

He got up on the bed on his knees and pulled his shirt over his head, tossing it to the floor. He reached back and took his shoes off one at a time, each falling to the floor with a thump. As he reached for and unfastened his slacks, I tried to prepare myself for what was about to happen. As he slid himself out of his pants, I figured myself lucky to have gone so long without this happening already.

My only hope was it wouldn't hurt too much. But even if hurt a lot, I would still be better off than Stephanie, Melinda, and Crystal.

And it was better to have this happen here, upstairs in a real bedroom, than in the torture chamber downstairs on the cold concrete floor.

Positioning himself between my legs, he lowered his body onto mine.

I tried to relax, telling myself that if I were tense, it would be more painful. But how could you relax while something like this was happening?

As he entered me, I was surprised. In fact, I gasped. Ron thought it was a gasp of pleasure, but it was surprise. I'd expected him to be rough, but he was gentle. He had never been gentle with the other girls, at least not that I saw. I had every reason to expect him to be forceful and fierce with me, but he wasn't. I'd been expecting a brutal rape like those that I'd witnessed downstairs, but instead, this was more like...well, more like lovemaking. In his mind, that's what it was. He was making love to me. But in my mind, it was still rape.

As he rocked my body, the images of him with the other girls flashed through my mind. The choking, the yelling out my name, the way he'd rammed himself against Stephanie's dead body. All of it entered my mind. I tried to push the thoughts away, and find a happy place.

I imagined myself on the beach. I felt the sand squishing between my toes. I could feel the water hitting my ankles. I could hear the sound of the waves and the seagulls. I could feel the warm sun beating down on me.

Before I knew it, it was over. He kissed me all over my face and left the room.

I lay there, feeling as though a huge weight had been lifted from my back. The thing I'd been dreading had finally happened, and it hadn't been so bad. And he was halfway through writing the book, which meant he was closer to possibly letting me go. Things were really starting to look up for me.

But of course, what goes up must come down.

\*\*\*

The next morning, Ron kept his word and brought me a few things to occupy myself with. He brought a book of word searches, a book of crossword puzzles, a crayon to write with, and a book to read. To my surprise, it was his first book. I honestly hadn't expected him to let me read it. But here it was.

After breakfast, he headed off to his bedroom to write, and I picked up his book, titled *Welcome*. The cover was reminiscent of a romance novel, except it depicted a man strangling a woman. Nothing romantic about that. I opened the book and began reading.

Hours later, I closed the book and yelled to Ron that I was hungry. He came in and made us each a bowl of soup. While we ate, he asked me if I was done with the book.

"Not yet. Almost."

"By dinner?"

"Yeah."

"Good. I can't wait to hear what you think about it."

"How's the other one coming?"

"Good. Everything's flowing nicely. I did hit a snag, however. Nothing for you to worry about, though. It'll all work out."

We finished our lunch and he rushed back to his bedroom. I hurried through my secret exercises and got back to reading the book.

It was no wonder the damn thing hadn't sold well. It was horrible. It was sloppily written. And the story—a group of lost hikers stumble across a shack in the woods in which a family of murderers live and are killed one by one (like that hadn't been done to death, no pun intended)—didn't hold up. The timeline was wrong, and the names were confused a few times. The people in the story did things that normal, real people could never do. They had impossible strength and their bodies were pushed far past the point that would've killed any human.

As I closed the book and thought about that, I realized that was why he tortured people in the basement. He was testing the human body for that realism he talked about. He needed to know just how far a person could be pushed before they fell. Just how far they'd bend before they broke.

I shuddered to think I was one of his subjects, even though I hadn't really been tested physically.

Then I gasped. He wasn't testing me physically. He was testing me mentally. He was pushing all my buttons, arousing my emotions and messing with my mind. He was seeing how far he could push me before I snapped.

Well I wasn't your average broad. I was a mother. I wasn't snapping that easily. If he wanted to break me, he had his work cut out for him.

As we ate dinner, Ron asked the inevitable question that I'd spent the afternoon preparing to answer.

"What did you think? And be honest, Nicole."

"It was interesting," I said.

"How so?"

"The things your characters did and how they interacted with one another were interesting."

"Did you like it?"

"Yes." I didn't.

"Did you think it was good?"

"Yes." It wasn't.

"What was your favorite part?"

The end, when it was over. "I kind of liked the ending. When the girl got away."

"Well, she didn't really get away."

"No. But she did for a minute. Until he caught up to her and dragged her back to the house kicking and screaming."

Studying me, Ron asked, "What would you have done differently had you been her?"

I was careful with my words. I didn't want him to know how I would do anything if I got away from him, because there would be a day when I did, and I didn't want him to know what to look for.

"I think she did everything right. She just got caught. He was smarter than her. She did all she could."

He kept staring at me and nodded, clearly satisfied. I assumed he was the man in the story, so saying that he was smarter than his victim was a stroke to his ego.

If I guessed it right, Ron had sat around and fantasized about kidnapping and killing a woman. Or women. Instead of actually doing it, he'd written that book. However, the book was a flop. This gave him a reason to live out his fantasies for real, not just on paper.

Then again, I could be completely wrong. Maybe he was just a psychopath who enjoyed killing women and decided to write about it. His first book flopped, so he thought he'd write the next one as he tortured the women instead of later. After all, he had just told me that he wanted to write about Crystal while it was still fresh in his mind.

Either way, the man was nuts. And his book sucked.

That night, after he handcuffed me to the headboard, he kissed me goodnight and left, saying he was going to write. I welcomed the darkness and the silence.

I fell asleep quickly and had horrible dreams. In them, Ron was having his way with me. Oddly, in my dreams, I enjoyed it. I moaned and moved beneath him as he rocked me steadily. As he brought me to climax, I threw my head back, arched my back, and opened my eyes.

I was shocked to discover that it was real. It wasn't a dream. Ron was on top of me, naked and panting, and I was in the throes of a soul-shaking orgasm. I tried to stop it, but I was too far in. As my body tensed and spasmed, tears rolled from my eyes and dropped onto the pillow. I gasped and started to moan, but I bit my lower lip to stop it from happening. I couldn't stop the orgasm, but I could stop the moan. Or so I thought. It still managed to escape me, though not as loudly as it would have otherwise. That was the most bizarre orgasm I'd ever had.

How could this happen? How could I have let it happen? I felt disgusted.

Minutes after my orgasm, Ron had one of his own. He quickened his thrusts and finally trembled on top of me, shuddering to a stop. He lay on top of me for a few minutes, kissing my neck as his breathing returned to normal.

"That was amazing, Nicole. Absolutely amazing." He got up, kissing my breasts as he went. He grabbed his clothes and left me in the room alone, in the dark, crying, racked with even more guilt.

I felt like I'd cheated on Wade. I was so angry at both Ron and myself. Was it normal? Did it happen to other women? I had no idea. It was one of the many things I'd have to ask the psychiatrist that I'd no doubt be seeing for years after I got out of this house.

The one thing that kept coming to my mind was would Wade be angry with me? Would he forgive me or feel as though I'd cheated on him? I knew that he'd be so happy to see me alive he wouldn't care about that and wouldn't hold it against me. It wasn't cheating. I was held captive by a madman who had forced himself on me while I slept. My dream state had tricked me. It's not like I went out and got myself a boyfriend. He would know that.

But why did I still feel like I'd betrayed him?

# 17

**M**any days later, Ron left the house, saying he had several errands to run. He said he would be late getting back and that he'd pick up dinner while he was out. Discussing what dinner would be, we agreed on a pizza and he left.

I sat at the table, doing word search puzzles, one after the other. It successfully kept my mind occupied until Ron returned with the pizza. To my surprise and dismay, he brought more than just a pizza.

He walked in, smiling, and set the pizza on the table. He also had a brown paper bag, which he set on the floor beside his chair.

"Miss me?" he asked.

"Like an ingrown hair," I replied.

He laughed and took two plates from the cabinet. As he set them on the table, he said, "I have a surprise for you, Nicole."

"Yeah? What is it? A dead puppy?"

He chuckled, as usual. "No. It's better than that. But it can wait until after we've eaten, don't you think?"

"If you weren't going to give it to me until after we eat, why'd you mention it now?"

"To tease you, of course." He smiled and served us each a piece of pizza and a soda.

We ate in silence for a while. I wasn't sure what he was thinking, but I was wondering what sort of surprise he could possibly have for me.

As soon as we were finished, Ron cleared the dishes from the table, put the remainder of the pizza on the counter by the refrigerator, and put our soda cans in the recycle bin. It still struck me as funny that a serial killer as twisted as Ron would recycle, but I'd seen him do it many times. Newspapers, aluminum cans, and plastic bottles. He was a saint except for that nagging killing thing.

Ron returned to his chair and leaned over. I heard the bag rattle. He sat up straight, but didn't show me what he had for me.

"Have you enjoyed your stay here, Nicole?"

"Are you serious?"

"Of course I'm serious."

"I'd rather be at home."

"I know you would. But have you enjoyed your stay here?"

"It hasn't been as bad as it could've been, I guess."

He nodded. "I've brought you something I think you will enjoy greatly. It's a little reward for behaving so well while you've been here. I made a stop while I was out today. I had to tell a little white lie."

"As opposed to a big black one?"

He crunched his brows together. "What was that?"

"Nothing," I said, shaking my head.

"Anyway, I know you've been here a while and I thought I'd do something nice for you. So I stopped off and got you this."

He brought his hand up from his lap and placed the item on the table. When he pulled his hand back, I gasped.

"Where did you get that?" I demanded.

"You sound angry."

"Where did you get that?"

"Well I didn't get it from a store."

"Where?" I said through clenched teeth, trying to keep from crying.

"Let's just say it's used."

"You son of a bitch. Tell me where you got that."

"I think you know, Nicole."

117

I cried. I reached out with my left hand and picked it up. I slowly brought it up to my nose and inhaled deeply, breathing in a scent I hadn't smelled in months. It was the wonderful scent of my beautiful baby boy.

"I see you recognize it as belonging to your son."

I nodded.

"I thought you might."

Struggling to control my emotions, I said, "It's his first teddy bear. It's one of his favorites."

"That's sweet," he said without emotion.

"How did you get this?" I asked, thinking he'd broken into my house and stolen it.

"I took it before I left."

"What do you mean before you left?"

"Well as Wade was leading the way to the door as I left, I picked it up."

"Wait. You talked to Wade?" I couldn't believe it.

"Yes."

"Why? I don't understand?" And it was clear that he didn't want me to understand.

"I rang the doorbell and Wade answered."

"Why were you at my house?" I didn't disguise my anger with him. I couldn't.

"I wanted to see the people you love. Maybe figure out why you love them."

"Did you see Mason?" I hoped he said yes, and I hoped he said no. I didn't want him around my son, but I wanted to know if he was okay.

"Yes. He's really a very cute baby. Wade isn't bad looking either. Am I a better lover than him, Nicole? Be honest."

This was one of those questions to which there was no right answer. Either way I went, I was undoubtedly walking into a trap.

"Nicole? Am I?"

"You're different."

"Good different or bad different?"

"You have a different style than he does." I hoped that would satisfy him enough to shut up about it. The truth was I hated Ron and his touch. When I thought about him being inside me, I cringed.

When I thought of his spunk spilling into me, I nearly vomited. It disgusted me. I'd never felt that way with Wade.

He didn't look as though my answer was the one he wanted to hear, but he did move on to other things.

"Wade seems to have moved on."

"What?"

"Yes, he didn't mention you once while I was there. He didn't cry. Didn't as much as sniffle while I was there, which was every bit of half an hour."

"Maybe he didn't want to show his feelings to a stranger."

"Maybe. Or maybe he just doesn't care about you anymore."

I shook my head. "He cares." I knew he cared. Nothing this asshole could say to me would change my mind about that.

"I don't think so. There was no shrine built to you or anything. Like I said, he didn't seem sad to me. I'm sure he's moved on. It's been a long time, after all."

"It's your fault that I'm not there with them, like I should be." I fought to keep my voice even, but it was a battle I barely won.

"Do you not want to be here?"

"Of course I don't want to be here. I thought I made that perfectly clear from the first day. If I wanted to be here, I would've come over, rang your doorbell and asked if I could stay. You wouldn't have had to drag me here with a gun to my ribs."

He nodded. He left the room and went to the basement. I didn't know what he was doing down there and I didn't give a damn. I was pissed. He'd crossed a line when he went to my house.

I closed my eyes and sniffed the little brown bear with the red bow around its neck, breathing in the marvelous aroma of baby. My little Mason, with his daddy's blue eyes and cheek dimples. I cried silently, wishing more than anything that I was home with him, bathing him, feeding him, rocking him, and singing to him. I longed to feel Wade's arms holding me as I held Mason.

Come hell, high water, or an angry Ron, I was going to see them again.

*** 

Sometime later, Ron returned to the kitchen to find me sitting there, staring at the puzzle book, but not doing the puzzles. My mind was on my son and husband. I held the bear close to me, clutched tightly against my chest as if I was drowning and it was a life preserver.

"Are you glad I brought it here?" Ron asked.

I shrugged. I didn't know what he wanted me to say and frankly, I was tired of always guessing what the right thing to say was. It was mentally exhausting.

"Well, Nicole," Ron snapped. "Would you rather I bring Mason here?"

I jerked my head up and looked at him, my heart racing. As much as I wanted to see, hear, and hold Mason, the thought of him being trapped here with me was unbearable. Even the thought of this psycho touching him was enough to make me furious.

"You leave my family alone. Don't you ever go to my house again, and don't you ever touch either of them." I tried to keep my voice even, but it came out higher than I wanted and frantic sounding.

With more than an ounce of arrogance, Ron walked over to me and leaned down, hands on his knees. Eye level with me now and only a couple feet away, he spoke with an iciness I hadn't heard before. At least I hadn't heard him speak to me this way.

"I don't think you're in any position to be barking out demands to me, Nicole. Now I enjoy your feisty attitude more than anyone, but you're walking a fine line now between an adorable feisty attitude and a nasty insubordinate one. I don't think you want to be insubordinate. I think you want to be the cute, feisty girl I fell in love with and play nice."

I don't know if it was the way he was talking to me as if I were a child or the tone he used, or maybe it was him saying he was in love with me, but for whatever reason, before I knew what was happening, I reached out and slapped him with my left hand. Had my right hand been free, I'd have punched him in the mouth. But my aim wasn't as good with my left hand, so all I could do was slap him across the cheek.

Instantly, his face turned red. Not from the slap so much as from the anger that exploded in him. His eyes narrowed and I swear they darkened.

"How dare you?" he spit at me, his words heavy and menacing.

"How dare me?" I asked, finding my voice. "How dare you?"

120

He stood and began to pace frantically back and forth across the kitchen.

"I bring you into my home. I treat you well. I give you everything you want, everything you need. I make love to you. I spend time with you. And this, this is how you thank me. With your infantile behavior and your smart mouth. You're ungrateful, Nicole. Ungrateful!" He stepped toward me as he shouted, then stepped away from me and continued to pace.

"I don't want to be here," I yelled at him. My body trembled as I stepped across the line I knew I was crossing. I was in dangerous territory and for some reason, I couldn't make myself shut up.

He stormed over to me and quicker than I expected, he backhanded me across the face hard enough to nearly knock me out of the chair.

"You bitch," he screamed.

He quickly and roughly unlocked the cuff from the table and forced me to stand. He dragged me down the hallway, squeezing my wrist so hard I couldn't feel my fingers, and causing me to drop the teddy bear. I tried to resist. I planted my feet and tried to pull against him, but we were moving so fast, I barely had time to plant my feet, much less get good leverage to take a stand.

"Stop," I said.

He responded by yanking on my arm hard enough to cause a considerable amount of pain. I quickly followed him.

He pulled me quickly down the hallway and into my bedroom. He shoved me onto the bed and locked the cuffs around the headboard.

While he cuffed me and roughly yanked off my jeans and panties, he said through clenched teeth, "If you want to act like one of those bitches in the basement, I'll treat you like one."

After he'd nearly ripped my panties off me, he unfastened his pants, took his position, and went at me fiercely.

With my eyes closed, I tried to block it all out, tried to pretend I was somewhere else. If I could separate my mind and body, it wouldn't be so bad. And for the most part, I was successful. I imagined I was elsewhere, on the hammock on the beach, but I was still aware of the pain he was inflicting on me. I was still aware of the anger inside me from knowing that he'd been in my house and in contact with my family.

I was also aware that he was having some trouble. He was yelling and cursing at me. It seems he was having trouble having an orgasm. Good. I hope he never had one again.

When his erection began to fail him, he sat up on his knees and wiped his face roughly with his hands. His chest heaving with his heavy breaths, he glared at me. His mean stare was making me feel really uncomfortable. He'd never looked at me this way before.

He pointed at me and said, "You. It's your fault."

Before I could ask what he meant by that, he reached down and slapped me across my left cheek. It was my turn to glare at him.

He slapped me again, this time a backhand to the right cheek.

"You son of a bitch," I shouted. "Stop hitting me."

"You like being a basement bitch?" Another slap.

"Knock it off, asshole!"

He smiled. Then, he slapped me again.

My face was stinging terribly on both sides. I wished my hands were free. If they were, I'd punch him in the throat.

Then I realized that although my hands were cuffed, my legs were not. Even as I moved, I knew I was making a huge, stupid mistake. But I couldn't stop myself.

As he held up his hand to slap me again, I brought my legs up, planted my feet on his chest, and shoved with all my strength, sending him flying off the end of the bed and to floor, where he landed with a heavy thud.

My heart was racing. That was so stupid. Now what was I going to do? I couldn't flee. I couldn't fight him back.

He stood, slowly appearing over the foot of the bed. He wiped his mouth, and I saw blood on his hand. He must've bitten his tongue or his lip. Wow. I sure could make a bad situation worse.

He looked at me now with a look that made the previous look seem like a charming grin. In his eyes, I saw hatred. He no longer found me charming and wonderful and great company. I was certain that he despised me. Maybe he wouldn't always, but he sure did right then.

He smiled wickedly and climbed back onto the bed.

I learned a few things that day and in the days that followed. If I fought him, it turned him on. It drove him harder. Regular sex with me wasn't enough for him anymore. He needed the thrill of a fight.

He needed to hit me and have me struggle. Just like the girls in the basement.

This frightened me. It hadn't taken him long to grow tired of me sexually. He found a horrible way to be interested in me again. How long would it take him to bore of me this way? And worse yet, what would the next step be?

# 18

My next period brought me some peace. It meant that for a few days, Ron left me alone. He could rape a woman—alive or dead, he could torture and dismember bodies all day long, but he couldn't have sex with a woman while she was menstruating. Well, even Superman had Kryptonite.

Usually, when I had my period, he still sat at the table with me and had dinner and played cards. Everything was the same. But this time was different. After he made our meals, he set my food on the table in front of me and took his to his bedroom.

He barely spoke to me. The conversations were minimal at best. We didn't play cards or have drinks.

As much as I hated to admit it, I was lonely. It wasn't that I liked him or even liked having him as company. The problem was that without him to keep me occupied, I grew sad. I thought of my situation more. That meant I dwelled on Wade and Mason and what would happen if I didn't make it back to them. I could've easily fallen deep into a depression, but I fought it. I tried to keep myself thinking about what Ron was doing in his room. What his book was going to be like. Different ways I could escape if I could ever get out of the cuffs.

On the third day of my period, which was definitely the heaviest, I sat at the table, having just finished my lunch. Ron came in to return his plate and glass, and to take mine to the sink. While he washed the dishes, he spoke. It was the most he'd said to me in days.

"I'm going out for a while. I'll bring back a pizza if you want."

I had noticed his tone was flat and emotionless, but I pretended not to. "Yeah. That'll be fine. How long will you be gone?"

It took him so long to respond, I was sure he wasn't going to. Finally, he said, "I don't know."

I wanted to ask him if he was going back to my house. But I didn't. I didn't want to anger him, especially at this point. I had a terrible feeling that I was only an inch away from being shackled in the basement. Also, I was afraid he'd say yes. I couldn't sit here and wait, knowing he was with my family. It would kill me.

As it turns out, it killed me to sit there and wonder if he was at my house just as much as if I'd known he was.

Ron left and I sat at the table doing word search puzzles. After completing ten puzzles, I grew tired of word searches and switched to crosswords. After five of those, I needed to pee.

Squeezing my legs together, I continued to sit at the table. I had no other choice. I tried to do another crossword, but lacked the concentration. All I could think of was waterfalls, rivers, creeks, and dripping faucets. Damn.

I thumped the crayon on the table rapidly. Then, in a lame attempt to take my mind off my urinary needs, I tried to thump out the tune to a song. A drummer, I am not. I failed miserably, cussed loudly, and put the crayon on the table roughly.

My feet bounced on their toes, making my legs bob up and down quickly. It helped for a while, but soon enough, I was thinking again about peeing, and the bouncing legs only jostled my gorging bladder.

Putting my left arm on the table, I rested my head on my arm and closed my eyes. Eventually, the urge to pee subsided. I still had to go, but the feeling let up a little. Now I could concentrate on my wrist, hanging in the handcuff, barely touching my right thigh.

I opened my eyes and looked at the shiny cuff on my wrist. I hated it. Turning my arm slightly, I looked at the keyhole and wondered what all I could stick in there that would possibly open the lock. Even if I came up with a long list of items, it wouldn't matter. I couldn't get my hands on any of the things that might unlock the cuff. The only place I was ever allowed any sort of freedom was the bathroom. And the only things in there were a toothbrush, a comb, and some other hygiene items.

Looking at the hole, I had an idea. If I broke a tooth off the comb in the bathroom, maybe I could hide it in my pocket and later use it to try to open the cuff. I wasn't a criminal. I was a lock-picker or a locksmith. To be honest, I didn't even know how the lock on the cuffs worked. But I had to try something. I made a mental note to try it.

Then the urge to pee came back.

I sat up and spent the next ten minutes trying to pull my hand out of the cuff. I had some success, if you count chafing the skin and bruising the bone where my thumb attaches to my hand.

As my hand fell to my thigh, my eyes welled with tears. I fought them back, determined not to cry, not to let the situation get the best of me. But just when I thought I couldn't be any more uncomfortable, my situation got a whole lot worse.

I felt it. I held my breath and prayed that I was wrong, but a second later I was certain. Sticky warmth spread between my legs. My tampon had failed me. It had done all it could, but in the end, was unable to last until Ron decided to return. Damn him for leaving me like this.

What felt like at least an hour went by and the urge to pee was painful to say the least. I'd done all I knew to do to fight away the urge. And when I lost the battle, as my bladder released itself onto the chair and spilled onto the floor beneath me, I damned him for putting me in this predicament.

I cried now. I had no reason not to. My situation was hopeless and only getting worse. I was covered in blood and piss and still handcuffed to the table. I couldn't get away from the smell or the man who caused this whole mess. I cried hard, letting the sobs rock my body.

Exhausted, I stopped crying.

Surely he'd be back soon. He'd been gone a long time now. I had no way of knowing exactly how long, but it had been a long, long time. The sun was low in the sky now, casting a dark orange glow in the kitchen through the window over the sink. I watched some dust speckles dancing in the glow of the fading sun and wondered how much longer I'd have to sit here before Ron came back.

As it turned out, I had to sit here until the sun was completely down and night had fallen. The room was too dark to do any puzzles, so I just sat in the chair, staring at nothing, listening to the hum of the refrigerator.

By the time Ron flipped on the light, I'd fallen asleep with my head on the table. When the light came on, I opened my eyes and sat up.

I looked at Ron, who put a pizza on the counter and grabbed two plates from the cabinet. He turned to face me, one plate in each hand, and stopped when he saw the mess. After staring at the mess, then up at me, he brought my plate and set it on the table in front of me. Though I wanted to stomp away in anger and demand he tell me where he'd been and yell at him for leaving me sitting here like this for so long, I was hungry. So I picked up the pizza.

"It's cold," I complained as I took a bite.

Ron said nothing. He looked at the mess again before taking his plate to the other side of the table and sitting. I was surprised that he was sitting at the table with me, but in my present mood, I didn't give a damn.

"You've made quite a mess," he finally said between bites.

"I believe you made this mess," I snapped.

"I didn't urinate all over my kitchen floor."

"No, but you left me here for hours. What did you expect to happen?"

"I expected you to exercise control over your bladder."

"And I expected you to exercise common sense. You should've known I couldn't sit here for that long without using the restroom."

"You should've waited."

"You should've hurried."

He stopped chewing and stared at me. That was bad. But when he nodded as if he was agreeing with some inner voice (which he probably was, the crazy bastard), it was worse.

127

Now I sat there in my mess, eating cold pizza, wondering what he had in store for me and hoping that I never found out.

*\*\*\**

After Ron allowed me to clean myself up, he cuffed me to the bed. I slept well, having exhausted myself while sitting at the table earlier.

The next morning, Ron led me to the bathroom, where my new clothes were waiting. I suppose he didn't want to clean the blood and urine from my panties and jeans, so he'd gone out and bought me some. That was fine. My other ones were getting worn pretty thin. Just like my nerves. And my mental state.

I did everything I had to do in the bathroom, including wondering if a string of tampons tied together would be able to choke a man to death, and snapping a tooth from the comb and sticking it in my left front pocket. Had I put it in my right pocket, I'd never have been able to retrieve it. He always cuffed my right hand, probably because it was so awkward to use my left. It was surely his way of keeping down escape attempts. He was clever that way.

I stepped out of the bathroom and faced Ron, who still hadn't returned to his old self. He was still cold and distant, but really, what else did I expect of a psychopathic serial killer?

Ron grabbed my arm, cuffed my wrist, and led me to the basement.

Trying to sound as if I weren't terrified, I asked, "Why are we going down here?"

"I think you have lessons yet to learn, Nicole. Don't you agree?"

"No, I'm good. I'm pretty sure I've learned enough." I tried to sound light, as if we were just having an ordinary conversation. As if I wasn't afraid to find out what lessons he had in mind.

I'd assumed he was going to put me back on the mattress. But he didn't. Instead, he sat me in the chair and handcuffed my arms behind me, around the beam. When he moved away from me, I noticed Crystal. This was the first time I'd seen her in a while, and she looked awful. Beyond awful. She looked so terrible there wasn't a word to describe it.

But there was a word to describe her baby bump. Larger. Somehow, the baby had managed to grow inside her. I didn't imagine she was eating. She certainly didn't look like she'd been eating. She was stick-thin.

Ron walked to the cabinet to retrieve whatever implements of torture he desired. While he was across the room, I called to her quietly, but she didn't hear me. I saw her breathing. I knew she was alive, but she didn't respond.

"Crystal," I whispered louder.

"She won't answer you," Ron said, turning to face me.

I watched as he walked over to her, cattle prod in his hand.

"Is she okay?"

"Does she look okay, Nicole? Really, you can be so ignorant at times. It's disappointing and unbecoming of you."

"Oh, I'm sorry," I said as sarcastically as possible. "Did I make you think less of me? You, the psychopath. Thinking less of me, the victim. Bizarre, isn't it?"

"Is that how you see yourself? As a victim?"

"It's what I am."

"We are all defined by the way we see ourselves, Nicole."

"Oh yeah?"

"Yes."

"Well I see myself at home, snuggled up with my husband and son." I looked around, eyes wide with feigned shock. "That's weird," I said. "I saw myself one way, but that's not the way I am at all. So odd."

"There you go again, Nicole."

"There I go again what? Showing you how stupid your way of thinking is?"

"No, there you go again, proving up your ignorance. There's no need to continue proving yourself, Nicole."

"Are you calling me ignorant?"

"If the shoe fits." Before I could call him all the bad names I had in mind, he spoke again, this time turning the conversation towards Crystal. "Crystal, wake up." When she didn't respond, he nudged her in the side with the toe of his shoe. When she didn't respond the second time, he kicked her in the ribs.

She moaned.

He smiled. "There you go. Wake up and say hello to Nicole. She hasn't seen you in a while. But today, your special day, she came. We both agreed that she should be here, and we knew you'd want her to be here as well. Isn't that right, Crystal?"

She didn't respond.

He stuck the cattle prod to her and shocked her to screams. It may have not been so bad if he'd put it to her belly or leg, or anywhere other than where he did. But he put it on the worst spot possible. Where there had once been a tattoo. A tattoo that he'd carved away, filling the remaining hole with salt.

From my position, I could see the hole, swollen and an angry shade of red. It was obviously infected, and the shock that he sent through it had to hurt like hell. Only a monster would do something like that. I looked at him as he shocked her wound and knew I was right. Only a monster would do something like that. And his name was Ron.

# 19

When Ron had finished torturing Crystal by shocking her infected wound, he turned to me.

"Do you see, Nicole? Do you see what's going on here?"

"If you're talking about the psycho with the shock wand inflicting damage on an innocent pregnant woman who can't defend herself, then yes. I do."

I saw the anger wash over him. Then, I watched as he stomped over to me and stuck it to my chest, between my breasts.

My heart was racing. I held my breath, unsure of what to expect. I clenched my teeth and stared into his eyes, waiting for the pain to come, but it didn't.

"I'd be sure I was prepared to reap before I started sowing, if I were you, Nicole."

After staring me down for a minute with the cattle prod pressing against my breastbone, he walked away. He went back to Crystal.

"I don't think you understand me fully, Nicole. I think you believe you can toy with me and nothing will happen as a result. It's painfully obvious that your parents never taught you that for every action is an equal and opposite reaction."

He squatted down between Crystal's spread legs.

My heart pounded harder. My palms grew sweaty behind me. I felt nauseous.

In his right hand, Ron held the cattle prod. As he aimed at Crystal's private area, I was afraid he was going to shock her there. That would be bad for the baby. It had to be.

"What are you doing?" I nervously asked, trying to either buy time to think of something else or make him forget about her. "How is that an equal and opposite reaction to anything that I've done? And by the way, what is that I've done?"

He threw me a hateful look and said in an even more hateful tone, "You bled on my chair. I had to clean that up. Do you know how horrible that was?"

"Are you serious? Do you know how horrible it was to bleed on your chair? And then to sit in it for hours? It's your fault. Besides, I've seen you clean up some pretty nasty stuff down here. I would've thought you were used to it."

"Used to it doesn't mean I like it." He took a few deep breaths to calm himself down. He looked back at Crystal. "But since you bled on my chair, I'm going to make her bleed."

"Wait," I said quickly. I couldn't believe what I was about to say, but I had to say it. "Why make her bleed? I bled on you chair. Make me bleed."

"No."

"Why not? That's the only fair way to do it."

"Damn it, Nicole. Would you shut up? I don't want to make you bleed. I want you to feel bad because she's bleeding because of you. That's the punishment. Making you bleed would only hurt you for a little while. Making her bleed because of you will make you hurt forever."

And with that, he plunged the cattle prod into Crystal's vagina.

I screamed no, but he couldn't hear me over her. Once he turned it on, her body jerked and spasmed as she yelled and gurgled. I thought he'd pull it out and stop, but he didn't. He kept it in her, kept shocking her.

"Stop," I screamed.

If he heard me, he gave no indication.

As her body stiffened and shook, her heels and elbows scraped across the concrete, leaving red stains on the floor. Her right breast rolled out of the way at one point and I had a clear shot of her infected wound. It was worse than I'd thought earlier. There was a large area that was dark red, but worse than that, there were areas that were black. I could even see the pus from this distance. I was sure it was worse than just an infection. If she survived the basement, she would surely lose a large amount of flesh.

Finally, Crystal stopped jerking around, but the yelling didn't stop. Ron yanked the cattle prod from her vagina and cursed as the blood dripped from the tip of the prod, falling to the concrete with a splat.

"Damn batteries," he said. He jumped up and ran over to the cabinet in a frantic search for more batteries.

"Crystal, are you okay? Can you hear me?"

Nothing came from her except yells and moans. When the yelling began to taper off, I was relieved that her pain was coming to an end. Little did I know that her pain was only beginning.

As I lowered my head and wept silently, Crystal began to scream. Assuming Ron had replaced the batteries and was shocking her again, or maybe brutally removing some of her other tattoos, I looked up. But he was still at the cabinet, fumbling around in his search for batteries.

I watched as she screamed and wondered what sort of agony she was going through, simultaneously hoping I would never find out.

"Damn it. Well," Ron said, returning to Crystal sans cattle prod. "Since I don't have any spare batteries, we'll just have to do things the hard way."

I saw the knife as he brought it up and ran his finger slowly along the blade. He glanced at me to make sure I was looking. I was. I'd stopped crying, but the tears on my cheeks were still wet.

"Aw. Don't cry yet, Nicole. Cry later, when I've finished with her."

"Please stop," I begged. "I won't make any more messes, and if I ever do, I'll clean it up. I swear. You don't have to do this to her."

"Actually I do have to do this."

"No, you don't." Before I could tell him that I'd learned my lesson, he spoke.

"Yes, I do. It's not all about you, you know. The whole world doesn't revolve around you, Nicole. Don't be self-centered. It isn't fitting to you. I've reached a slow spot in the novel. I need a little spice. This will serve two purposes. It'll teach you a valuable lesson, and it will help me liven up the story."

"Novels are fiction. Fiction means fake. You can make it up, Ron. Please leave her alone."

"Made-up stories don't sell."

"Uh, yeah they do. Every single day."

"Well not mine. My book was fake, and it didn't sell. This time, though, it'll be a bestseller. Why? Because it's going to be real. It'll be believable. And I owe that to you, and the other women."

He squatted down beside Crystal's torso and watched her face as she screamed.

He waited until her screams became sobs before he set to work, carving away the tattoo above her other breast. Her sobs quickly returned to screams.

Unable to watch him slicing through her flesh, I looked away. That's when I saw the rapidly growing pool of blood gushing out from between her legs. Dark red blood ran out of her and across the floor toward the drain.

I gasped, but over her screams, no one heard me.

"Ron," I said, but he didn't hear me. I couldn't look away from her blood. I knew what was happening. It was inevitable, but it still shocked me to actually see it. "Ron," I yelled over the screams.

He looked at me, frustrated at being interrupted.

"She's having a miscarriage," I said, nodding toward the blood.

He looked at the steady stream of blood coming from her and smiled. The son of a bitch smiled. I couldn't believe it. Well, I guess I could. What I couldn't do was imagine how anyone could smile at such a horrible thing.

I watched as he went back to removing her tattoo, paying no more attention to her miscarriage.

He carved.

She screamed.

I cried.

The baby died.

As if I needed another reason to hate Ron, I now had one. It was bad enough that he tortured and killed women, but to kill an unborn baby and smile about it was an unspeakable act of evil. Had Crystal not came into contact with Ron, she would've had the baby, and the baby could've grown up and lived a full life. Now it was dead, having never fully developed.

The fact that Ron smiled when he saw what he'd done was just a further testament to his capabilities. I don't know what I'd expected of him when I'd pointed out that she was losing the baby. Maybe I expected him to be shocked, or at least to look sympathetic and sorry. A man who could smile at causing a woman to miscarry a baby was capable of anything.

And he was about to show me some more of what he was capable of doing.

When Ron had finished slicing away her tattoo, he held it up. A piece of skin slightly bigger than a half dollar dangled between his thumb and forefinger, dripping droplets of blood onto Crystal's neck. He turned to me to see if I was watching. Unfortunately, I was. Satisfied that his audience was captivated, he turned back to Crystal. He dangled the piece of tattooed flesh inches above her face, which was twisted in agony.

"You shouldn't mar your body in such a way, Crystal," he said, slapping the piece of meat against her cheeks. "Tattoos make you look trashy. They're vile and disgusting. And worse, they're permanent. Well, they're usually permanent. You're lucky I came along and removed them, aren't you? Aren't you?"

Crystal continued to scream, though her voice was weakening.

"Answer me," he screamed at her.

Angered that she wouldn't answer his ridiculous question, he grabbed her jaw roughly with one hand. Ron shoved the flesh that was formally connected to her chest into her open mouth, mid-scream.

Crystal's scream cut off and became a muffled moan as Ron held her mouth closed. She struggled as much as she could, but it was no use. Ron wasn't letting go. He held her mouth shut tightly with one hand and held her head steady with the other. With his face only inches from hers, he stared into her eyes as he spoke to her.

"Eat it. You wanted it on your body; you wanted it to be a part of you forever, so eat it. Make it a part of you forever. Swallow it down. It's part of you, Crystal. Just eat it! Swallow it." Screaming at her wasn't going to make her swallow it.

My stomach rolled and twisted in my belly as I watched her wrestle with him, a piece of her own flesh in her mouth.

Several minutes went by with Ron holding her in this position. Finally, he let go of her jaw and slowly pulled away his hands from her face.

I watched her carefully, so when she spat out the tattooed meat, I saw it shoot up out of her mouth and fall to the floor next to her. Quickly, I looked to Ron. His face turned red, his eyes narrowed, and I saw his jaw clench.

"You filthy whore," he said as he slapped her across the face.

I watched as he picked up the meat and once again shoved it into her mouth. She resisted, keeping her mouth shut tightly as long as possible. It wasn't until Ron stuck his finger into the hole in her chest where the meat had been just minutes earlier that she opened her mouth. It was to scream, but it was open nonetheless and Ron used the opportunity to shove in the flesh.

This time, he held her mouth closed for at least ten minutes. I started out counting, but after counting to sixty three times, I started thinking maybe it had been four times, and while trying to sort it out in my head, I lost track. But my best guess was at least ten minutes.

Finally, he sat up. She didn't spit it out this time, and Ron smiled.

"That wasn't so bad, was it?" he asked.

She answered his question by once again spitting the grotesque wad of meat out and onto the floor, this time, above her head.

I was afraid he was going to punch her, kick her, slap her, or choke her. In fact, judging by the look on his face, I wouldn't have been surprised to see him beat her to death.

But he didn't. When he got done with her, she'd wish he had beaten her to death, but that's not what he did.

With his left hand, he grabbed the nipple of her left breast. He pulled it, stretching it upward until her breast became elongated.

As I tried to determine what sort of punishment this was, I found out.

Quick as a flash, Ron brought up the knife and slashed it through the air. It took a second for me to realize that he had not only sliced the air, he'd sliced through her breast, taking off the nipple and a good portion of the rest of it. When I noticed a third of her breast dangling by the nipple from between his fingertips, I looked down at what was left of her breast. It looked like an erupted volcano, blood oozing out of the opening and running down the sides like lava.

Her screams burst forth, filling the room and bouncing off the concrete walls.

Ron smiled.

He tossed her ruined breast to the floor and grabbed the nipple of the remaining breast. He stretched it upward, just as he had the other one. He again slashed the knife through her skin. This time, however, he didn't make a clean slice. He only made it halfway through.

I watched as he began to slowly saw back and forth with the knife through the rest of her breast, making jagged cut marks.

When I noticed the silence, I looked at Crystal and saw that she'd passed out. I was surprised she'd made it as long as she had without succumbing to the darkness.

When Ron finished cutting off her breast, he brought it to his face. I was sure he was going to take a bite out of it, or maybe drink some of the blood from it. My mouth began to fill with saliva in preparation of the vomit that was sure to come.

He brought it to his nose, inhaled deeply, and smiled. What a sick bastard.

He looked at Crystal, prepared to speak, but saw she was unconscious. Slamming the ruined tip of her breast down, he stood abruptly and stormed across the room to the cabinet.

I looked back at Crystal. Her breast had landed on her abdomen, making for a spectacle that seemed to have originated in a science fiction horror movie. Her breasts were chopped and bleeding, and on top of her swollen abdomen rose what looked to be a third breast, nipple reaching for the ceiling.

I felt horrible for her. All this because of me. No. It wasn't because of me. It was because of Ron, but he wanted me to think it was because of me. Even though it wasn't because of me, I was crying. I felt responsible. I should've done something to protect her.

When Ron came back from the cabinet, I begged, I pleaded, I cried openly, but it was no use.

Suddenly, things got a whole lot worse.

Ron dropped to his knees beside Crystal and set the tools of torture beside him.

"Wake up, Crystal." There was a threatening tone to his voice. It was as if he were saying 'wake up now and prevent what's about to happen'.

When she didn't stir, he nodded and began what can only be described as the most horrific thing I've ever seen.

As he removed the lid from a bottle with a label I recognized to be rubbing alcohol, I looked at the steady stream of blood that still made its way from Crystal to the drain. Only now, it wasn't just a stream. It was more like a small river. It was getting worse, and fast.

I looked back at Ron just as he poured a hearty amount of alcohol into the crater that was formerly Crystal's left breast. This brought her around in a hurry, which was obviously what he wanted. He wanted to torture her and inflict as much pain as possible on the poor girl, but he wanted her to be awake while he did it.

Her screams and wails were loud, but her voice was failing her. She'd done more screaming than any actress in a bad horror movie had ever thought of doing. It was wearing on her.

I couldn't watch. I closed my eyes and hoped Ron didn't notice. If he realized I wasn't watching, it would get worse for her.

I listened to her screams as her voice cracked and broke, and then fell silent. Hoping for her sake that she'd passed out again, I opened my eyes and checked on her. She was wide awake, still thrashing against her restraints, and screaming though no sound escaped her. Her voice had finally gone.

Tired of pouring alcohol into her open wound, Ron set down the bottle and picked up an ice pick.

"What's that, Crystal? I can't hear you?" he said.

He used his left hand to grab her right breast at the base. He squeezed it, making the bleeding mound of flesh rise farther away from her chest and jabbed in the ice pick. He jabbed it quickly up and down, as if he really was chipping away ice. Blood spattered across her chest and belly, along with pieces of breast meat.

My stomach rolled and a mouthful of sour spit overwhelmed me. Unable to take it any longer, I leaned forward, spread my legs, and vomited on the floor between my feet. I was aware that my mess-making was the cause of her agony, but there was nothing I could do about this one. I'd held it back as long as I could.

Ron must've realized that I wasn't looking.

"Nicole, are you watching? Are you making another mess?"

"I'll clean it," I said between retches.

"You need to watch this, Nicole. These are valuable lessons I'm teaching you."

"I can't. I can't watch anymore. Please stop. You're killing her."

"I'm afraid Crystal is killing herself."

"No, you are," I spat at him.

"I may be the tool, but she's the one behind it, instructing me."

"How can she instruct you to do anything? You've made her scream so much, she can't even talk now." I wanted to add asshole to end of that, but thought better of it.

"Her actions have spoken louder than any words she could've said."

I didn't know what actions he was talking about and I didn't feel like finding out. Though I'd thrown up, my stomach was still uneasy. I was trembling. My nerves were frayed. And the guilt was unbearable.

Tired of torturing a woman who couldn't give him pleasure by screaming, Ron stood.

"I think that's enough for the day, don't you?"

"Would you please take her to the hospital? You're going to kill her. She's dying right now. Please," I begged.

"That's kind of the point, isn't it? You know very well I can't let her go. I can't let any of them go. To let them live is to bring about my death."

We stared at each other for a minute, neither speaking. I didn't know what he was thinking, but I was hating every fiber of his being. I hated even the thought of his existence. All the ways I could kill him flashed through my mind as I looked into his empty eyes.

"Let's go eat breakfast, shall we? I'm famished."

As Ron unlocked the cuffs and dragged me up the stairs and into the kitchen, I wondered how the hell he could possibly be hungry after doing what he did. I'd seen it, and I didn't know if I could ever again eat a bite without seeing blood and pieces of meat behind my eyelids.

# 20

I sat cuffed to the table as Ron scrambled eggs, buttered toast, and poured two glasses of milk. When he set mine in front of me, I pushed the plate away and sipped the milk. My stomach was uneasy to say the least. There was no way I could eat. But he ate as if it were his last meal. Oh, how I wished it was.

Halfway through his plate of food, he realized I wasn't eating.

"Eat," he said around a mouthful of egg.

"I'm not hungry."

"Sure you are. Go ahead. Eat."

"How can you eat after seeing that down there?"

"Easy. Just don't think about it."

"How can you not think about it?"

"I just don't think about it. That was a few minutes ago. It's over. Besides, it was just blood. You of all people should understand that blood is natural."

"Why me of all people? What does that mean?"

"It means you weren't too disgusted to eat last night while you were sitting in a large puddle of blood, which by the way, I had to smell while I ate."

Weakly, I replied, "That was different."

"Not to me. Blood is blood."

Was that true? It couldn't be. It had been disgusting sitting in my blood last night. It was horrible and vile, and the only reason I'd eaten was I was starving.

As I rolled this around in my mind, I realized what the difference was. It wasn't the blood. If I would've just seen a bunch of blood, it would've been a different story. I would've still been able to eat if I was hungry. The sight of blood wasn't what made me lose my appetite. It was the cause of the blood. It was seeing Ron torture Crystal. It was watching him cut her and cause her to bleed that had made my appetite flee.

I continued to sip my milk. I was afraid Ron would get mad and cram the eggs down my throat. That reminded me of him trying to force Crystal to eat her own flesh. I shuddered and quickly thought of something else.

"What are you going to do after breakfast?" I asked, afraid of the answer.

After washing his food down with a long drink of milk, he said, "Write. That was some good stuff down there and I need to write it before I forget it."

"You could forget that?"

"No, but I want to write it while it's fresh. While all the details are still vivid. I will never forget it," he said as he smiled.

I wasn't going to forget it either, and I sure as hell wasn't smiling about it. I knew there would be many sleepless nights ahead of me, as well as many nights where I woke up screaming from a nightmare that was actually a memory.

And that's if I lived through this.

"You won't have another chance to eat until lunch. You sure you're not hungry?"

I shook my head.

"Mind if I eat it?"

I pushed the plate toward him. He pulled it the rest of the way to him and gobbled it down.

He washed the plates and glasses and walked down the hall to his room to write the atrocity that was his novel, leaving me cuffed to the table.

I did my exercises quietly, more to keep my mind off Crystal than anything. When I'd gone through my routine, I began doing crossword puzzles. I'd completed two puzzles and was halfway through the third when I remembered the tooth of the comb in my pocket.

My heart raced. I put down the crayon and looked over my shoulder to make sure Ron wasn't standing behind me or coming up the hallway. Seeing no one, I reached into my pocket and pulled out the tooth.

I dropped it. Then I picked it up. My nervousness was making me clumsy. I was excited with the prospect of being free. I closed my eyes and calmed down. A few deep breaths later, I was fine. Okay, so I wasn't fine, but I was calm enough to use the tooth without dropping it.

I stuck the tooth of the comb into the key hole on the handcuff. I wiggled it around, poking here and there. I had no idea what I was doing. I'd never picked a lock before. I didn't even know anyone who had picked a lock. I just assumed it would be as easy as it was in the movies where you could just stick something in the hole, jiggle it a little, and voila, it would open. But that wasn't the case. Or maybe I just did it wrong. Whatever the case, the cuff wasn't opening.

And then the tooth snapped in half.

Shit.

I looked at the short piece of plastic, grasped desperately between my thumb and forefinger. Had I really thought this would work? I put what was left of the tooth back in my pocket and sighed.

That had been my only plan. Now what was I going to do? Well, the only thing I could do at the moment was more crosswords. So I did.

I was still doing them when Ron came in to make us lunch. He stood at the counter and made sandwiches as I finished up a puzzle. As I put the crayon in the book and closed it, it hit me.

Where was the other piece of the tooth? What if Ron stuck the key in, realized something was wrong, and found the rest of the comb tooth? I think it would be safe to say that what had happened to Crystal was nothing compared to what he would do to me.

I made sure Ron's back was turned and looked into the hole on the cuff. It was hard to see. I had to bend down and get closer, turn my wrist so more light could get into the key hole, and squint to look into the small dark space. I saw nothing. Looking up at Ron to make sure he still wasn't looking, I shook my wrist, thinking maybe if I shook the cuff, the tooth would fall out. It didn't. I looked around on the floor but saw nothing.

Ron brought my sandwich and I ate, but all I could think of was the tooth. Where was it? If I couldn't see it on the floor, it had to still be in the hole. That meant the next time he unlocked the cuff, I was screwed.

\*\*\*

When Ron had returned to his room to write the great American novel, I shook the cuff, trying to free the piece of plastic from the keyhole with no success. Frustrated, I finally decided to ignore it. I didn't see it anywhere, and worrying myself to death over it was doing me no good. I put it out of my mind and tried to finish the crossword puzzle. Unable to concentrate, I switched to word searches.

We ate dinner that evening in silence. That was fine with me. I had images in my head that took all my strength to push away, and the broken comb tooth kept popping into my mind. There was quite a wrestling match going on in my head, and that left little room for forming sentences and holding a conversation.

As Ron washed our dinner dishes, I asked about Crystal.

"You want to know how she is? Let's go find out."

He released the cuff from the table and I breathed a sigh of relief that the tooth wasn't in the keyhole. He led me down the hallway, down the stairs, and into the basement where he sat me in the chair and cuffed my hands around me behind the beam.

I couldn't take my eyes off Crystal. She looked bad. And that was an understatement.

As I assessed the damage Ron had done to her, he walked over to her and nudged her with the toe of his shoe. She didn't move. While my eyes travelled down to the mess between her legs, Ron kicked her in the ribs. She still didn't move. As I noticed the amount of blood that had come from her and found its way across the floor to the drain, now mostly dry, Ron drew back his lower leg and kicked her with all his strength. She still didn't move.

143

While Ron stood over her, head tilted in confusion, I held my breath and stared intently at her chest, looking for the signs of life that I prayed were there.

I saw nothing. Her chest wasn't rising and falling as it should've been. She was dead.

Ron squatted beside her and felt her neck for a pulse. Apparently feeling nothing, he stood and placed his hands on his hips.

"Damn," he said.

"What?" I asked, as if I didn't know.

"She's dead." He sighed.

I looked at Crystal. It was probably better for her that she wasn't still alive. The psychological trauma of her situation would've been hard enough to live with, but even if she could've gotten past that, the physical damage would've been a painful reminder of what she'd lived through. Yes, death was a kind escape for Crystal.

But it didn't mean that I didn't cry for her. Two young lives lost, one before it even started. It was sad.

I hid my tears from Ron. I didn't think it would be good for me if he knew that her death had affected me in any way. So I sat there in the chair, hands cuffed behind me, and watched as he chopped her up just a couple feet away.

I jumped every time the axe found its way through her body and connected with the concrete floor beneath her. The sound of the metal hitting the cold, hard floor would be one that would haunt me for the rest of my days. And nights.

As Ron removed Crystal's arms and legs and put them in trash bags, I knew I had to get out of here. I couldn't take it anymore. I couldn't watch him hack up another body and keep my sanity. I couldn't watch him torture another woman. I just couldn't.

After Ron hauled Crystal's body up the stairs two bags at a time, he led me up the stairs.

He led me to the bathroom door and removed the cuff from my wrist.

I thought of running, barging past him and out the door. After all, he was probably tired from all the hacking and hauling of the body, and I just might be able to get away. But when I glanced at him, I knew that wouldn't happen. It would, however, cause him more hacking and hauling because I had no doubt that he'd kill me.

I turned and went into the bathroom.

I peed. I flushed. I washed my hands, scrubbing all the way to the elbow until my skin was red. I splashed cold water on my face. I looked at my reflection in the mirror above the sink, but I didn't see me. Instead I saw Crystal's lifeless, mangled body lying in the basement.

I rushed over to the toilet and threw up my dinner. After emptying the contents of my stomach, I flushed, stood, and went through the routine again of washing my hands, splashing my face with cold water, and brushing my teeth.

Having done all that, I opened the door and faced Ron, who filled the doorway.

He quickly slapped the cuff around my right wrist and led me to the bedroom. He undressed me, pushed me onto the bed, and cuffed me to the headboard as always.

When Ron left to dispose of Crystal's body, I cried.

# 21

The next morning, I woke to the sound of a slamming door. I opened my eyes and focused them just in time to see Ron barging into my room.

He stood in the doorway, chest heaving with angry breaths, eyes wide, hair disheveled. The sleeves of his white shirt were rolled up to the elbow which meant he'd been cleaning. I couldn't imagine what could've angered him while he was going through his cleaning routine, but he was obviously furious. Suddenly, I was very awake.

"You," he said. And that was all he said. Then, he rushed across the room and slapped me across the face.

"What the hell?" I yelled at him.

"What the hell? What the hell? I'll tell you what the hell," he yelled back as he angrily unlocked the cuff from the headboard.

He jerked me from the bed. Unable to get my feet under me in time, I crashed to the floor, knees first. I gasped and cursed at the sudden pain. This was no way to wake up. He continued pulling me along behind him, not giving me enough time to stand. I had to struggle to get to my feet as we rushed along down the hall toward the kitchen.

When he finally stopped and turned to me, I was suddenly aware that I was naked. He had a tight grip on my right wrist, but my left arm was free and I used it to cover myself as best as I could. I had little other than my dignity. And at this point, I was clinging to scraps of that.

He was only a couple feet from me. I could feel the angry heat coming off him.

"Is there something you want to tell me, Nicole?" he asked, his voice booming.

My mind raced to think of what he could be talking about. Unable to think of anything, I shook my head. "No."

"Really? There's nothing you want to say to me? Nothing you want to tell me about?"

I shook my head.

He nodded. "Alright then." And in a flash, he was jerking me down the hallway. He opened the door to the basement and pulled me down the steps. Immediately, my body tensed and I began to pull back, trying to remain upstairs. He responded by pulling harder on my wrist, leaving me no choice but to follow him.

"What are you doing?" I asked, not caring that even I could detect the panic in my voice. I hated the basement. Nothing good ever happened in the basement.

"Teaching you a lesson. Apparently, you like learning the hard way."

When he dragged me off the bottom step, I was sure he'd take me to the mattress. But he didn't. Instead, he pulled me away from the mattress, across the room, toward the shackles that were secured to the concrete floor. My heart froze in my chest.

As he pulled me past the beam that I normally sat against with my arms bound behind me, I reached out with my left hand and grabbed it. I held on with all my strength, which compared to Ron's, wasn't much. Barely noticing that I was using the beam as an anchor point, Ron gave me a tug and kept walking, unaware that my hand now contained several splinters of wood that stung my palm from the inside. How I longed for the days when a handful of splinters was the biggest worry I had.

When we reached the place I dreaded the most, Ron turned to me and said, "Get down on the floor."

"No way." I folded my arms across my bare chest, both in defiance and modesty.

"Get down, Nicole. Don't make me tell you again."

"I'm not getting down there. I don't understand why you're doing this."

"Stop lying," he screamed. I'd never heard his voice this loud or heard this tone come from him before. Clearly, he was beyond angry. And I think it was safe to say that I had crossed that line I'd been tightrope walking for so long.

"What do you think I'm lying about?"

"Shut up and get down on the floor."

"No," I said defiantly. What did I have to lose? He was hell bent on shackling me to the floor. I couldn't do much to resist, but I was going to do what I could. No sense making this easy on him.

"Nicole, you can do this the easy way or you can it the hard way. No matter which you choose, you're getting on the floor."

"Why?" I asked.

Then, everything got real dark real fast.

*** 

When I woke, I was alone. Still naked, I was cold. The left side of my face throbbed furiously with each beat of my heart. I couldn't believe Ron had punched me. All this time, I'd thought his liking me, or as he'd put it lately, his loving me would protect me from his wrath. Looking back now, that was a stupid assumption to make. I'd been a fool to assume anything would protect me from a psychopathic serial killer who suffered from mood swings.

Fully awake now, I realized that I was lying on the cold, unforgiving concrete of the basement floor. It was the same place where many women had died before me. Would I be next?

I tested my restraints. There was no getting out. The chains that were secured to the floor were thick. The shackles around my wrists and ankles were tight. Too tight. There was absolutely no way I'd be able to slip free of them. I was going to be here until Ron decided otherwise. And usually when Ron decided to let you go, you left via trash bags.

I tried not to think of that. If he really loved me, he wouldn't chop me up and dispose of me. Of course, even as I thought that, I realized it was silly. I couldn't depend on the love of a madman to save me. Madmen didn't know what love was. They didn't understand that you never, ever hurt the people you cared about.

I realized now how stupid I'd been. Shackled in the basement in the same place he'd tortured and killed numerous women, I still thought I could figure him out. I still thought his emotions were like those of normal people, and his affection for me would save me. Ron was right. I hadn't learned a damn thing.

With no choice, I waited for Ron to come to the basement. I kept myself occupied by thinking of Mason and Wade and all the things we'd do when I got out of this madhouse. I had so much to catch up on. They'd spent about five months without me. I wanted to hear all the details of their lives. All of Mason's firsts that I'd missed. I knew that Wade would want to hear all about what I'd been through, but I didn't want to tell him. And if I could help it, I wouldn't. He didn't need to hear this. I'd seen things that would curl the toes of hardened police officers and make their skin crawl. I couldn't put that on him.

At some point, I dozed off while thinking of Wade and Mason. I dreamt of them. The dream was so real I could feel them, smell them, and I could clearly hear them. I sat on the couch beside Wade, Mason on my lap. I smiled broadly at Wade as he leaned in to kiss me. Just before his lips touched mine, his mouth opened, revealing long, sharp teeth. Instead of kissing me, he sank those teeth into the soft flesh of my neck.

I vaguely became aware that the pain in my neck was more than just a dream. It was too vivid, too real to be a dream.

As I slowly opened my eyes, I saw Ron hovering over me. I blinked quickly a few times and cleared my mind. I had to be on my toes with Ron.

"Do you have something to tell me, Nicole?"

"I don't know what you want from me," I said calmly.

"All I want from you is the truth."

"The truth about what?"

"Everything. More specifically, anything you may have been keeping from me. A secret, if you will."

"I don't know what you're talking about. How can I have a secret? You know exactly where I am at all times."

"Apparently that isn't good enough."

"What does that mean?"

The sharp pain in my neck came again and I realized that whatever it was, Ron was doing it. He seemed to be poking me with something sharp.

"Last chance to tell me, Nicole. Then, things will get bad for you."

"Ron, I don't know what you're talking about. If I did, I'd tell you. I don't keep things from you. I couldn't if I wanted to."

"And now you're lying to me." He shook his head.

"I'm not."

"You are," he screamed.

He held up a short piece of plastic, the item he'd been using to poke at my neck. The same piece of plastic that I'd used to try to unlock the handcuffs. The broken piece of comb tooth that I'd been unable to find was now held tightly between Ron's thumb and forefinger. Somehow, somewhere, Ron had found it.

"Still sticking with that story, Nicole?"

"What is that?" I asked, trying to sound innocent.

"So you are. Well, that's your choice. Just know that whatever happens to you now is your own doing. I've given you more than a fair amount of opportunities to come clean and be honest with me, but you've chosen again and again not to. For whatever reason, you choose to cling desperately to your lies. And for that, you alone stand responsible for your fate."

I considered telling him the truth, but I figured it was too late for honesty.

He stood and walked away. It wouldn't have been so bad if he'd left, but he didn't. He walked over to the cabinet. That wouldn't have been so bad either if I hadn't known that inside the cabinet is where he kept his implements of torture.

Suddenly, I needed to pee. And puke. And cry. And scream. But I couldn't bring myself to do any of those things. I was too afraid to move.

With his back to me, Ron fumbled around in the cabinet. It sounded as if he were picking things up and sitting them down, probably trying to decide on which to use. I thought of turning my head to look, but decided I didn't want to know. If I saw the tools he was choosing, it would only make matters worse. Sometimes it's better to not know. That's why dentists always hold their tools down, out of the line of sight until sneaking them around your cheek and into your mouth. Dentists are in the know. And probably all five asked, not just the usual four.

I began to tremble.

Though I'd feared being in this position as I'd watched him destroy the other women, I'd never actually thought I'd be here. In my arrogant stupidity, I'd assumed his fondness for me would keep me from this spot. And now that I was here, I was terrified beyond words. Images flashed through my mind of things he'd done to them. And they were women who'd meant nothing to him. He claimed to love me. He felt he'd been betrayed by the woman he loved. So the very thing that I'd hoped would be my salvation, his love of me, was about to turn out to be my downfall.

I closed my eyes and wished with all my might that whatever he was about to do to me wouldn't be that bad. I started out wishing that he'd let me go, but I felt like that was a long shot, so instead I concentrated my efforts on the lesser punishment. As long as I could survive and live the rest of my life in peace after this, I'd be okay. But if he started slicing off my breasts, well, I didn't know how I'd handle that.

When I opened my eyes, Ron was standing over me.

Holding a hammer.

Shit.

"Ron, can't we talk about this?"

He squatted beside me. "I tried to talk to you, Nicole. Talk time is over."

"What are you going to do?"

"You'll see." Then he smiled at me. Had I had use of my hands, I would've ripped that smile off his face and shoved it up his ass.

He turned my left hand over so that my palm was flat on the floor. He placed his foot on the back of my hand at the base of my fingers. He put all his weight on it, causing me considerable pain. Of course, that was nothing compared to what came next. And somehow, I knew that's how it was going to be.

I stared at my left hand, but I couldn't see it because Ron's leg was in the way. His right knee was on the floor, his left foot on my wrist. I saw him bend over, and then I felt him messing with my fingers. The same fingers which were starting to go numb from lack of circulation due to his foot on my wrist cutting off the blood flow.

Unsure of whether I actually wanted to see what he was doing, I alternately squeezed my eyes shut and tried to see around his foot.

When the pain came, I was glad I couldn't see.

I tried to hold back, but the third time he hammered, I cussed loudly. I said every bad word I knew. I even invented some new ones.

After hammering five times, Ron stopped. He stood up. I looked at my poor hand.

The blood came rushing back to it, causing a pins-and-needles sensation that was agonizing, especially for my forefinger, where the tingling sensation faded into the background and was replaced by an intense throbbing. Lifting my hand off the floor as far as I could, I could see why that finger hurt more than the others.

The broken piece of plastic was about half an inch long. Almost every bit of it was buried under my fingernail. Nothing more than the very tip of it poked out from under my nail, which was cut off even with the tip of my finger. Blood ran from under the nail and slowly rolled down the side of my finger and into my palm. As it trickled its way down my wrist and under the cuff, I shot a hateful look to Ron.

"How could you?" I sounded pitiful. Even as I said it, I realized I was lucky. If this was all he done to me, I was thankful. I should stop bitching.

"You lied to me, Nicole. You're lucky that's all I did to you."

He turned to leave the basement.

"Wait," I said urgently.

He slowly turned to me as he stepped onto the first stair.

"Aren't you going to take it out?"

"No." He continued up the stairs.

"But it hurts," I whined, still aware that things could be so much worse.

"I know." With that, he shut the door at the top of the stairs, leaving me alone in the cold, damp basement, naked and bleeding from the finger.

I cried for a while, but finally decided to stop being a baby about it. I'd had worse pain. After all, I'd had natural child birth. But still, the tip of my finger throbbed ferociously with every heartbeat.

Ron must've found the broken comb tooth while sweeping. I hadn't been able to see it, but he'd found it somewhere and had known that it was because of me. Of course he'd known it was me. There were only two of us in the house and he knew he hadn't done it. It was painfully obvious that it was me. And when questioned about it, I'd lied to him. That pissed him off. It was funny how a psychopath who lived in a world of delusions could be so hell-bent on people being honest.

# 22

Ron left me shackled in the basement. Minutes felt like hours, and then became hours. Hours felt like days, and then became days. I had no way of knowing this. I could only guess at how much time had passed by the angry growl of my stomach and the amount of times I'd peed and defecated.

At first, I did a lot of thinking. I thought about my husband and son. I thought about my mom. I thought about everything I could possibly think about. When I'd exhausted my thoughts, I slept.

What started out as an escape from my boredom soon became a necessity. I was weak and growing weaker by the second.

My serious thirst was evident in more than just my dry mouth and guttural craving. I was urinating very little now and far less frequently. I held it as long as possible, pleading with my body to hold onto it and suck as much sustenance from it as it could. Eventually, I lost out and what little urine my body had produced seeped out of me, ran across the floor and dripped away into the drain, following the same route the blood of so many others had taken.

Along with the lack of urination, my defecation soon ceased. Taking in no food, I was producing no waste. That didn't mean that the waste I'd already produced wasn't still lying on the floor underneath me. I gave up the hope that Ron would come and wash it away. Apparently he wasn't going to.

Scary thoughts crossed my mind. What if something had happened to Ron? What if he'd been killed in a car accident and no one knew I was down here? How long would it be before anyone came? I tried to push those thoughts away before I succumbed to madness.

Instead, I thought of all the things I was going to do as soon as I got out of here. Because damn it, I was going to get out of here. As hard as it was to keep pretending that escape was possible, I clung to it with every fiber of my being. There had to be a way, and all I had to do was find it.

As I imagined myself soaking in a hot bubble bath, surrounded by lit candles and classical music, I fell asleep. I dreamed of water. Lots and lots of water. It started out as a babbling brook nearby, then turned to rain, and then became a raging waterfall. I tilted my head up and enjoyed the feeling of the water as it splashed off my neck and chest and against my face.

I slowly opened my eyes and realized that it wasn't a waterfall at all but a crazy man with a water hose.

When he saw me open my eyes, he didn't smile the way he used to. In fact, he didn't smile at all. He briefly met my eyes, and then looked away, continuing to spray around my body.

"You've made quite a mess down here, Nicole. I understand the urination and defecation, but what I don't understand is the vomit. Are you sick?"

Was I? I couldn't remember throwing up. I vividly remembered feeling sick at my stomach because I still was.

I tried to speak, but my mouth was too dry. I closed my mouth and wiggled my tongue around in a futile effort to work up some saliva to coat my mouth and throat. It was no use. My body was too dry to even make spit.

Ron must've seen this. "You thirsty?"

Had I been able to talk, I would've called him some of the new cuss words I'd invented as he'd hammered a splinter of plastic under my fingernail. But all I could do was nod.

He aimed the hose at my face, particularly my nose and mouth. I had to turn my head to avoid drowning. While he laughed, I let my mouth fall open and allowed the steady gush of cold water to pour in. It tasted like old, dirty rubber, but it was delicious. I swallowed until he moved the hose.

"Better?" he asked.

"Yeah," I said hoarsely. "How long have I been down here?"

Continuing to spray the floor around me, he said, "Five days."

"Why'd you leave me down here so long?" I wanted to yell and scream, but my throat was sore, and the words came out no more than a husky whisper.

"I needed some time away from you. I planned to leave you down here a day or two, but I got so wrapped up in the novel, I lost track of time. I might still be in my room writing if it weren't for my physical needs."

"Physical needs?" I assumed he'd been eating and using the restroom over the past few days.

Tossing the hose to the floor beside me, he stepped over to me and I suddenly knew what physical needs he was referring to. With the water streaming from the hose beside me, Ron unfastened his slacks and took his position between my legs.

Before I could begin to fathom how anyone—psychotic or not—could be aroused and feel okay about taking advantage of someone in this position, the nausea overwhelmed me and I vomited, though it was no more than water and stomach acid. I turned my head to the side and let it run out of my mouth as Ron went at me frantically.

Having sex on the floor was uncomfortable. Having sex on a concrete floor was worse. Being raped on a concrete floor while naked was the worst. Ron was putting everything he had into this, slamming himself against me furiously. His forceful thrusts had slid me on the concrete, creating scrapes on my backside. The shackles holding my feet were pulled taut now, and with each of his thrusts, the chains jerked my ankles and caused stabbing pains in my hips. Eventually, every inch of my body was hurting in one way or another.

He grunted in frustration. Occasionally, he stopped and repositioned himself.

After a while, he said, "Damn it."

He stopped, sat back on his heels, ran his fingers through his hair and wiped the sweat from his face. While he struggled to control his ragged breathing, he stared at me.

Deciding to give it another go, he forced himself into me again. He stared into my eyes. When it was apparent to him that just slamming into me wasn't going to bring him to orgasm, he wrapped his right hand around my throat and squeezed.

When his squeeze became tight enough to restrict my airway, I started to struggle. I jerked my head back and forth, desperately trying to shake his hand off my neck. I gasped for air and tried to scream. He laughed and continued going at me, seeming to enjoy it now.

As he grew closer to climaxing, his grip around my throat tightened and my vision grew dark. When he closed his eyes in ecstasy, I closed mine in submission, both welcoming Death and hoping he would pass me by.

\*\*\*

I was shocked awake by the cold water hitting my face. I opened my eyes and turned my head. Ron was standing beside me spraying me again with the hose. Up and down he went, spraying my body.

"You're a pretty dirty girl, Nicole," he said while he sprayed me. "We've got to keep you clean." He walked down and stood between my legs, spraying my private area. "We need to keep this clean, now don't we?"

I'd thought I was cold before, but lying on a cold wet concrete floor while being sprayed with cold water made me rethink it. I was freezing. My teeth were starting to chatter.

"Please," I managed to say between teeth chatters.

"Please what?"

"Let me go."

"Let you go?" He stopped spraying me.

I nodded.

"You want to go?"

I nodded again.

"Where do you want to go, Nicole?"

"Home," I said, my teeth clicking harder.

Ron threw down the hose and stomped away, toward the cabinet.

I closed my eyes and hoped he was just going to turn off the water. When I opened them, I saw that I was wrong. He hadn't turned off the water. What he had done was retrieved the knife. The same knife he'd used to carve my name into other women's flesh. The very same knife he performed mastectomies with.

The dim light of the bare bulbs bounced off the shiny blade and briefly illuminated Ron's eyes as he turned the knife around in front me, making sure I saw it. When he saw my eyes fall to the blade, he smiled. Not the usual smile he gave me. This was an evil smile. The smile of someone about to do something bad. Something very bad.

"Nicole, you know what I'm starting to think?" When I didn't answer, he yelled, "Do you?"

I shook my head slowly, which took all my waning strength.

"I'm starting to think you don't love me. I'm starting to think you don't even like me. Only someone with no heart could not like someone like me. Wouldn't you agree?"

I nodded slowly, feeling that this is what he wanted me to do.

Ron slowly lowered the knife to my chest. I thought he was bluffing. Even as I felt the tip of the long blade poke into my cold flesh I thought he was bluffing. I was certain he'd say something he found to be clever, and then he'd stop. But I was wrong. It seemed I was always wrong.

He sliced into me and I screamed. I didn't want to, but the pain was terrible. It was sharp and it burned, making any paper cut I'd ever had seem like lotion on the skin. He made two cuts that crossed each other in the middle, forming an X between my breasts. When he was done carving on me, I lay crying and shivering.

"If you ever make me think you don't love me again, I'll open you up right there," he said as he tapped on the cut with the bloody blade. "Where X marks the spot. And I'll find out if you have a heart or not. Do you understand that?"

When I failed to answer quickly, he stuck the tip of the knife in the center of the cut where the two lines met and twisted it.

I nodded.

"Good."

He got up and used the hose to rinse the blood from the blade. He returned the knife to the cabinet and finished hosing me down.

When the water filled the open cuts on my chest, the burning intensified and I cried harder.

When Ron felt he'd sufficiently cleansed me, he turned off the water.

My entire body trembled uncontrollably. My teeth clanked together loudly.

I was so caught up in my agony, I didn't notice Ron digging around in a dark corner of the basement. It wasn't until he turned it on that I realized what he'd been doing. He'd dug out a fan, plugged it in, and set it on the floor at my feet. It blew air up and over my body, making me colder than I already was.

"Can't leave you down here wet, now can I?" He smiled and turned to leave. At the bottom of the steps, he said, "I'll be back soon." At the top of the steps, he said, "You'll be happy to know that the book is coming along nicely. I'll be finished in no time. Isn't that great?"

I planned to nod in response, but he didn't wait for an answer. He turned and walked through the door, leaving me freezing and bleeding on the basement floor.

# 23

Cold. It was so cold. My muscles had been tense with shivering for so long, they ached and knotted up in spasms. My teeth clanked together so hard, I was sure they'd shatter at any moment. I couldn't feel my toes. I could barely tell that I was wiggling them, which made them ache and throb angrily. It's the only way I could remind myself that they were there.

The only good thing about being so cold was it numbed my skin just enough to ease the burning and stinging sensation radiating from the open wound on my chest. I still couldn't believe he'd cut me. He'd actually cut me. If I wasn't so worried about starving, thirsting, and freezing to death, I would've spent more time contemplating that. But as it turns out, I had more important things to worry about.

I drifted in and out of consciousness. At this point, I welcomed the darkness. When I was unaware of my situation, I could escape the pain. It was the only time I could.

Having no way to keep track of time, I wasn't sure how many days passed before Ron came back. As much as I hated to admit it, I was glad to see him.

"Nicole," he said and nudged me with his foot the way he'd done all the others before me.

I slowly opened my eyes, afraid that if I didn't, he'd deliver one of those hard blows to the ribs he was so fond of giving the ladies.

"You look terrible." He stood over me, soaking me in with his eyes. Finally, he shook his head and squatted beside me. "It's a shame. Such a shame it had to come to this."

I thought he was going to kill me. I almost hoped he would just to end my suffering.

But he didn't kill me. Instead, he began releasing my wrists and ankles from the shackles. Had I not been so close to death, I would've kicked his ass and ran. But I could barely roll my head to the side, much less fight or run. It took all my strength to blink, which I had to do because I sure couldn't keep my eyes open for more than a few seconds at a time.

"You've really took a turn for the worse in the four days since I saw you last."

Four days? That meant I'd been in the basement nine days total. Nine days without food. Nine days with almost no water. Nine days.

As he picked me up and carried me up the stairs, I caught a glimpse of my legs draped across his arm. My skin was a pale shade of blue. I looked up at him. I wanted to kill him. But more urgently, I wanted to eat. And drink. And sleep.

When Ron stepped into the hallway, I expected the warmth of the house to rush over me, but it didn't. Or if it did, I couldn't feel it. My skin was numb. He looked at me lying in his arms and asked, "Do you need to use the restroom?"

Though it took all my strength, I shook my head.

"Do you want to shower?"

I tried to shake my head again, but didn't have the strength. I managed to whisper, "No." I guess he heard me. He carried me to my room. Before he could put me on the bed and cover my bluish body, I'd closed my eyes and welcomed the relief that came with the darkness.

\*\*\*

When I woke, I wasn't sure where I was. I didn't recognize the room. It took a few minutes for me to remember the situation I was in.

The sun shone through the window and fell across the bed brightly. I lay there for a while, unmoving. My stomach wasn't really rumbling anymore. It was aching. All of my insides ached. My mouth was so dry, I was sure that if I moved my tongue, it would stick to the roof of my mouth.

Faintly, I could hear Ron across the hall clicking away at the keys of his computer.

Deciding to call to him, I tried to lick my lips, but it was no use. In fact, calling to him was no use either. My tongue was dry as a bone and so was my throat. Maybe that was why my voice refused to work. An ungreased wheel won't roll.

It was too much work, too much effort. I just couldn't do it. I closed my eyes, exhausted.

The next time I opened them, the room was orange with the angry glow of the setting sun. I didn't hear the clicking of the keys anymore. I wondered where Ron was. I considered calling to him, but remembered my previous failed attempt and pushed the thought away.

As I closed my eyes, ready to give myself back to the peaceful sleep I longed for, I heard Ron come into the room. Slowly, I opened my eyes again and looked to Ron, who stood beside the bed looking at me.

"Finally." He sat on the edge of the bed and reached out to the bedside table where a pitcher of water set. He poured a glass.

He put one hand behind my head and lifted it slightly off the pillow. He put the cup to my lips. I tried to make my lips purse to the cup to drink, but they were dry and stiff and refused to cooperate. So Ron slowly poured a little water into my mouth through my slightly parted lips. The water was cold and marvelous. My throat was too dry to swallow, so I opened my throat and let the water slide down.

It hurt at first, but felt good after that. I didn't drink too much. I didn't want to vomit.

"I'll be right back," said Ron after returning the glass of water to the bedside table. He left the room and returned a few minutes later with a small bowl and a spoon. He sat on the bed again and scraped the spoon through the bowl. He brought it to my mouth. "It's applesauce. It'll be easy on your stomach and won't hurt to swallow."

He was right. It didn't hurt to swallow, though the acid stung. I didn't even care about that. I just wanted more.

After feeding me, Ron left and I slept. It was an uneasy sleep, though. I periodically woke up, stomach racked with cramps.

Finally, morning came and with it, Ron. He came in and gave me water, which I was able to swallow. He fed me more applesauce, which I was also able to swallow. I was happy to learn that I could lick my lips without breaking them, though my upper lip did split in the middle the first time.

"Do you feel better today?"

"Yes," I managed to say. My throat was sore, but at least it worked today.

"Good. You had me worried."

I wanted to remind him that it was his fault. I didn't have the energy to say it, and I had the wisdom to know that it was a bad idea anyway.

As Ron got up, claiming he had to get back to his book, I asked to use the bathroom.

"Sure," he said. He released me from the bed and had to help me stand. As much as I hated it, I had to lean on him to walk to the bathroom. I'd never been so weak in all my life.

When we reached the bathroom, he opened the door and flipped on the light.

"Do you need me to come in and help you?"

I considered it. I probably did need his help. But I needed my dignity and pride more.

"No. I'll steady myself against the counter."

"Okay. If you need me, call out. I'll be right here."

I walked into the bathroom and Ron closed the door behind me. Wobbly, I sat on the toilet. I closed my eyes as the dizziness came and went. Though I'd felt like I had to pee a bucketful, barely anything came out. It was reassuring to know that my plumbing still worked.

After wiping and flushing, I made my way to the sink and washed my hands, taking care with the forefinger of my left hand. I opened the drawer and picked up my toothbrush and toothpaste. After squirting a glob of paste on the bristles, I brought the brush to my mouth and looked in the mirror. I froze at the sight of myself.

I knew I looked terrible, but I wasn't prepared to actually see myself in this condition. Having seen the other girls in the basement, I had an idea of what to expect. But to see it was a shock.

My hair was greasy and dirty, hanging in stringy strands. My skin was pale and blotchy. My lips were white and cracked. My eyes had large, dark circles around them. Gone were my round cheeks, replaced by sharp cheekbones.

Bracing myself for the worst, I let my eyes fall downward, taking in my still-naked body.

My collarbone was much more visible than it had been. In fact, all of my bones were more prominent, stretching my skin tautly.

And then there was the cut. Between my breasts was a large, rugged X cut into my flesh. Worse than the cut was the large red area around it, a sure sign of infection. And if the angry red area surrounding the cut wasn't enough of a sign of infection, there was the pus. I brought my left hand up to touch the wound, but noticed my finger.

Ron had removed the piece of plastic from under than nail, but an infection had settled in there too. And my nail had turned black.

I closed my eyes and brushed my teeth.

# 24

After helping me back to bed, Ron left, getting back to his book. I slept, the trip to the bathroom having drained me of my strength.

That's how the next couple days were spent. I ate and drank more each time, and soon began going to the bathroom with frequency. Eventually, I conjured enough energy to take a bath. I didn't trust my legs to hold me for a shower. Besides, sitting in the hot water helped shake off the chill I'd had since being in the basement. I'd just started to think I'd be cold forever, but the bath helped bring my body temperature back to normal and made me feel better.

A couple of days later, I was tired of lying in bed. When Ron came in carrying a small plate of scrambled eggs, I told him I wanted to eat them at the kitchen table.

He nodded and helped me to the kitchen, where he cuffed me quickly to the table and set my eggs in front of me along with a cold glass of milk.

After I'd eaten the scrambled eggs and drank the milk, Ron washed the saucer and glass. While he washed, he spoke.

"You're going to love this novel, Nicole."

I doubted it.

"It is a beautiful work of art that I can't wait for you to read. It will blow you away."

I didn't think so.

"I'm in the editing stage right now. It won't be long. By dinner this evening, it should be finished. I'm sure you've been waiting to read it."

I hadn't.

"I'm sure it makes you happy to know that all our hard work has finally paid off."

It didn't.

"Do you think it'll be good?" he asked, turning to me and dried his hands on a towel.

I shrugged. "I guess we'll have to see."

He nodded. He walked over to me, leaned down and kissed my forehead. He then leaned toward my ear and whispered, "I'll visit your room tonight to celebrate." Then, he walked down the hall to his room. Soon, I could hear the faint clicking of the keys as he edited his magnificent book of horrors.

For a while, I just sat there, happy to be out of bed but feeling sluggish. It was similar to the feeling I always had the day after I had the flu. My muscles were stiff and achy, and my head felt like it was floating away from my neck. I seemed to be moving in slow motion. But at least I was out of the basement. And alive.

A few days ago, that was something I was sure I'd never be able to say.

But here I was, cuffed to the table with a full albeit achy stomach, and I was alive. I just might live to see my son again after all.

I sat there for a long time, thinking. When I grew tired of thinking about everything except my time in the basement, I began to think of what had happened to me while I was down there. I didn't want to. But the memories kept pricking my brain, fighting their way in.

To keep my mind occupied, I decided to do a few puzzles. I looked around, but I didn't see either of my puzzle books.

I reluctantly called out to Ron.

"What is it, Nicole?" he asked as he came down the hallway.

"Could you get me one of the puzzle books?"

166

"Sure," he said walking over to one of the drawers. He brought me both puzzle books and a new crayon. "Is that all you need?"

"Yes. Thank you."

"Are you okay in here or do you need to go back to bed?"

"No. I'm fine."

"Okay then. I'll be in my room putting the finishing touches on what can only be described as a masterpiece. Call if you need me. Otherwise I'll see you in about an hour for lunch."

Ron left me sitting at the table doing puzzles. After three word searches, I put down the crayon and rubbed my eyes.

More out of habit than anything, I checked the cuff around my wrist. It was something I'd been doing since the beginning of my captivity. I'd always felt that there would come a day when he failed to tighten the cuff around my wrist, or a day that my wrist would be small enough to slide out, or a day when both of those things happened.

A day like today.

As I pulled my wrist slowly through the cuff, not all the way— just enough to make sure it would come out, I heard Ron clicking the keys on his keyboard, writing of his sins.

My heart pounded in my chest.

I stared at the shiny silver cuff loosely wrapped around my right wrist. Glancing over my shoulder to make sure that Ron was still in his room, I slowly and carefully pulled my hand from the cuff.

Instead of letting the cuff fall and risk it clanking and bringing Ron, I lowered it carefully and made sure it wasn't going to swing and hit anything. Then, I used my left hand to cup my right wrist, rubbing it gently in disbelief. I couldn't believe it.

I stood, careful to not make a sound, and walked lightly to the door that led from the kitchen to the laundry room. I went through the laundry room and into the garage. To my surprise, my car wasn't there. I don't know why, but I had expected it to still be there, hidden from the world. As I walked through the empty garage, I realized my car was probably at the bottom of the Mississippi River, still hidden from the world. Or maybe the bastard had taken it back to the mall to be found by the police, adding to the mystery of my disappearance by making them wonder if I was really missing or had just left to start a new life.

My heart was thumping so hard in my chest, it made my breathing fast and raspy, as if I'd been running.

I stood at the garage door, hand prepared to pull it open, but I hesitated. What if it made such a clatter that Ron came running and grabbed me before I could get out? I considered going back through the house and out the front door, but I was standing at a door, and that was an opportunity I couldn't pass up. I'd just have to be fast, which in my weakened condition, was asking a lot of myself.

I braced myself and pulled with all my strength as fast as I could, planning to get through the door and out before Ron had a chance to hear.

But instead of the door rising, it stayed put. My shoulder however, was a different story. I'd jerked suddenly with all my strength on a heavy door that hadn't budged. My shoulder now ached and burned. I'd obviously torn something. Adding to my new list of miseries was my chest. The scab that had formed on the X had pulled apart in my failed attempt to open the door. I could feel something running down my chest and abdomen. Blood or pus, I wasn't sure. But it didn't matter. This close to freedom, none of it mattered.

Realizing that this door was locked, I quickly went back into the house through the laundry room. I hated to, but I had no choice. There was no other door in the garage and I had to get out, even if it meant going back in.

Quietly, I stepped into the kitchen. I looked at the chair in which I always sat and shuddered as a chill ran down my spine. I looked to the hallway, checking for Ron. He wasn't there.

As quickly and quietly as possible, I crept through the kitchen. Where the kitchen and the hallway met, I turned, heading into the living room. I could see the front door and I focused on it, making it all I saw.

Over my raspy breathing, I heard nothing. That is, until Ron said my name.

I froze, my breath caught in my lungs. My mind raced, taking in many things at once. Closer to the kitchen than to the living room door, I felt my best chance was to get back to the chair. If I rushed toward the door, I'd never make it. Especially if it was locked.

Quickly, I retreated back into the kitchen where I sat in the chair.

Just as my ass hit the chair, Ron's voice boomed from the hall-way. I turned to face him. He was standing in his room, head and shoulders leaned through the doorway and into the hall.

"Nicole? Why didn't you answer me?"

Controlling my breathing as best as I could, I said, "I didn't hear you."

I thought I saw his eyes narrow with suspicion, but from this distance, it might've been my imagination. I couldn't be sure.

"I asked you what you wanted for lunch."

"Oh. A sandwich is fine," I said, trying my best to sound nor-mal.

"Ok. I'll be there in a second."

He disappeared back into the room and I quickly slipped my hand back into the cuff. I fought every instinct to do so, but I man-aged. After all, I'd spent months trying to pull my hand free, waiting for that one moment when it slid free, and that moment had finally arrived. Only here I was, having to slide my hand back into the cuff.

My freedom, having only lasted a minute or so and not even being actual freedom, had made me feel alive for the first time in months. Adrenaline was coursing through my veins, giving me a rush that no heroin junkie had ever achieved. I really was hopeful that I would make it through. How could I not be with the end so near in sight?

Ron came in and made us each a ham sandwich and a glass of iced tea.

Sitting across the table from him knowing that I could get free was intense. I had to make sure to appear that all was normal, but I was excited. My heart was pounding painfully in my chest. My hand trembled, but I didn't think he noticed. I kept it hidden in my lap as much as possible. My only real worry was that in my excitement, my cheeks would flush and he would be suspicious.

Fortunately, he had excitement of his own that kept him from noticing such things. I listened to him drone on about his monster piece, but all I could think about was opening the front door and running away, running back to my husband and son.

To keep myself calm, I didn't give much thought to the reunion. I could only think about one step at a time. Right now, the first step was getting through lunch. After that, I had to get out of the house.

When I was away from Ron and safe, I could think about other things. To be sidetracked now would be the end.

When we were finally finished with lunch, Ron washed our glasses. He then turned to me.

"Do you need anything else?"

I shook my head, afraid that if I opened my mouth, my voice would crack and give me away.

"Okay. I'm going back to my room. You'll be happy to know, Nicole, that in no more than an hour, my novel will be finished. And this is only the beginning." He smiled as he walked toward me. "We're destined to be together forever now, Nicole."

My blood ran cold.

"This book is the tie that binds us. Forever. I can't wait for you to read it." He leaned down and kissed my forehead. I fought back the urge to vomit, but I took some comfort in knowing that he would never be able to kiss me again.

I listened to the sound of his footsteps retreating down the hall over the sound of my furiously beating heart. My palms were wet with nervous sweat and trembling in anticipation.

When I once again heard the sound of clicking keys, I glanced over my shoulder to make sure I didn't see Ron. Then, I yanked my wrist from the cuff and stood on wobbly knees.

Without hesitation, I headed for the living room. But then I stopped.

I quickly and quietly walked back across the kitchen to the refrigerator. I reached up and grabbed Mason's teddy bear. Ron had stolen it from my baby and brought it here, sitting it atop the refrigerator as a constant reminder to me that he could take away my family at any time. There was no way I was leaving it here. Tucking the bear under my arm, I made my way back to the living room, where I raced to the front door.

First, I tried the knob. It was locked. I unlocked it. Then, I turned the knob and pulled on the door. It didn't open. I realized the deadbolt was locked. I unlocked it and once again pulled on the doorknob. The door opened.

I burst through the open doorway and into the crisp fall air.

As fast as I could, I ran down the front steps and across the lawn, my bare feet pounding the cold, hard earth as I went.

There was no house to the right of Ron's, only an empty lot. To the left was an abandoned house, windows and doors boarded over. Directly across the street, I saw no vehicles and assumed no one was home. But the house next to that one had a car in the driveway so I ran to it. With my left hand, I held down the doorbell button, and I pounded the door with my right hand. I kept this up until the door opened.

# 25
# One Year Later

I walk out of the store with a bag of groceries in each hand and head for my SUV. I'm halfway down the row of cars when a van pulls into the spot beside my vehicle. I freeze. I wait a moment, but no one emerges from the van. I turn around and go back to the front of the store where I sit on a bench and wait forty-five minutes for the van to leave.

Seeing no vehicle parked around mine now, I walk all the way down the row of cars until I reach my SUV. I put the sacks of groceries in the backseat, looking around to make sure no one is close to me. I then get behind the wheel and immediately lock the doors. Only then can I breathe a sigh of relief.

I drive straight home, checking my mirrors to verify no one's following me. Our new house is only a few blocks from the grocery store, so I'm home in minutes. Before getting out of my SUV, I look around to see if anyone is nearby. Seeing no one other than the elderly gentleman next door sitting on his porch, I get out and quickly grab the groceries and head inside the house, immediately locking the front door behind me.

Putting the groceries away, I realize the milk is warm and the butter is soft. It's not the first time I've had groceries go bad while waiting for a vehicle to pull away from mine. But I can't help it. I'd rather have food ruin than risk being kidnapped again.

\*\*\*

I stand at the side of the baby bed looking down at my son. He's a beautiful baby. He lies there, wiggling and cooing, and he reminds me of Mason at that age.

As if he can hear me thinking of him, Mason giggles in his bed. I turn around and smile at him and he closes his eyes, finally submitting himself to sleep.

I look back at my new son, Austin, and I can see no traces of Ron. At least not yet. I'm hoping I never do. I'm hoping against hope that he'll have all of my features and habits, and that he won't grow up to be a serial killer. I'm not sure that's how it works, but I'm keeping my fingers crossed.

Taking the baby monitor with me, I leave their room and walk into the family room. The drawer in the entertainment center catches my attention, calling out to me as it always does. This time, I give in and walk over to it.

As I watch my hand reach out for the handle, I ask myself if I'm ready. Is Dr. Brown right? Is it time to face it so I can move on?

I pull open the drawer and there it sits, staring up at me just as it has for the last three weeks, waiting patiently for the day I can finally bring myself to read it. Apparently, that day is today.

Reaching in and picking up the book, I tremble. Not just my hand, but my whole body shudders slightly. I close my eyes and tell myself it's over, even though I know it isn't. How can it be over when he knows where I live? We've moved four times in the past year, and yet Ron still knew where to send the book. I don't think it'll ever be over. As long as he's out there, it won't be over. And he is out there, somewhere, managing to evade police.

The book feels heavy in my hand.

I carry it with me as I perform my nightly routine of checking the alarm and every window and door lock in the house. Satisfied that the house is a fortress, I walk into my bedroom, where Wade is already in bed reading a magazine.

He smiles at me and I smile back.

I carry the book with me as I walk around the bed. Wade sees it. His smile fades a little, but he says nothing. I can feel him watching me as I crawl into bed beside him and turn on the lamp on my nightstand.

I smile at him and kiss him on the cheek to let him know it's okay. We've been talking about this for three weeks. We both knew I was going to read it. We just didn't know when.

Once I've settled in, I grasp the book firmly in both hands, trying to hide the trembling.

Wade places his magazine on his nightstand and scoots closer to me, putting his arm around my shoulders for support.

I close my eyes and take a deep breath, hold it, and let it out slowly. I open my eyes and look at the book.

Across the top of the cover in big, bold white letters is the word HELD. Across the bottom, also in big white letters, was his name, R.D. Redwine. Between the title and the author's name, is a picture that turns my stomach. It's a basement. A mattress lies on the floor, a pair of handcuffs dangling off the edge. I know this place well. I hid rotten dog food under that mattress. I spent a lot of time wearing those handcuffs. And the things I saw in that basement…

I shudder and fight away the tears that want to come.

I run my fingers across the raised letters of the title and take a deep breath. Unsure I'm ready, I open the book.

The dedication page reads simply: To Nicole.

At the bottom of the page, Ron has handwritten a message to me in red ink.

### The tie that binds us. Forever.

My eyes fill with tears, but I blink them away. I have no doubt that I'll cry more than enough when I'm finished reading this horrible book, this masterpiece of a madman.

I turn the page and begin reading.

Stepping out of the store, she squinted against the glare of the bright afternoon sunlight...

The End

Made in the USA
Las Vegas, NV
07 January 2022